Breaking the Tiger

by

Garey Riester

ESCAPE ARTIST
PRODUCTIONS
EASTON, PENNSYLVANIA

Breaking the Tiger

Breaking the Tiger

Breaking the Tiger is a contemporary, action-drama that takes place in modern-day India. Three characters--TESS DOUGLAS, a renowned CNN reporter; her cameraman and sometimes lover, DYLAN JENNINGS; and her new lover, the mysterious JAMES GUARDIAN-- speed recklessly down the fast lane of violence, money, sex and international intrigue into the black-market web of the skin trade and terrorism.

A dramatic, romantic triangle, explicit in its violence, suspense and political intrigue, transitioning between Tess's nightmare of an assignment gone bad in Iraq and her and Dylan's desire to find and save MAYA, a thirteen-year-old who along with twelve other abducted girls, may be the decoy for the possibility of a terrorist event that could become one of humanity's worst nightmares.

This poignant, emotional and riveting drama deals with the brutality of war, poverty, and trafficking and addresses the corruption of cultural morals that ultimately suppress and enslave millions of young women worldwide.

Introduction

In the last 30 years, I have completed 12 scripts and am still working on four others and have written five art history-related books. Several scripts I have worked on as novels. I have entered my scripts into many film and screenwriting festivals, becoming a multi-level finalist and award winner in 24 festivals, such as Houston, Beverly Hills, Amsterdam, Los Angeles, New York, Boston, etc. I have had two options, but neither made into films. I also had representation through the Gersch Agency in New York.

Through this, I continued to make my art and publish books like my art memoir, *Garey Riester: Strategies of Being*.

It is customary and an unwritten law that a writer does not attach any photos, not even a cover image, to their scripts. I have decided to change that. In my head all these scripts have been made into films. I know the actors I would like for each role. Examples: Walden Goggins and Sam Rockwell in *Escape Artist*; Jennifer Connelly in this script, *Searching for Asia*; Kate Winslet and Jon Hamm in *Breaking the Tiger*, Timothy Ollyfant, Tom Hardy, and Christin Park for *Bone Hunters*, fun to dream.

When films become hits, scripts are published with photos from the films. I have decided to publish my scripts, add a cover image, and images I have created throughout the text.

I am still hoping that my writing will make it to the big screen. If there is any interest in any of my storylines and/ or screenplays, please contact me at g_riester@aol.com or Garey Riester Escape Artist on Facebook.

Enjoy.

FADE IN

SUPER - EXT. - JUNGLE FOLIAGE - DAY - NORTH OF MUMBAI

A disheveled van sits alone in front of a tangled web of iridescent multi-layered, green jungle foliage.

INT. WEATHERED MIMI VAN - CONTINUOUS

A small, bare-breasted female figure riding a tiger hangs from the rear view mirror.

On the other side of the front window, orange cables run over the hood of an SUV with the Discovery Channel logo on passenger door.

PASSENGER SIDE OF VEHICLE

DYLAN JENNINGS, handsome, in his mid 50s, camera held on his shoulder, wearing Ray-Bans, a Yankee cap, and a Ramones T-shirt circles the van.

A YOUNG INDIAN MALE, REMI, attacks the cables, pulling them loose and off the hood of the vehicle.

                              DYLAN
          Let's go, gentleman. This is your dot-head fifteen minutes.

                         DYLAN (CONT'D)
          Tess!

The lush foliage separates and TESS DOUCLAS, attractive, in her mid 40s, shoulder-length hair, wearing a dark cotton jacket, jeans and well-worn boots, walks into the frame.

Behind Tess walks MAYA, a 17-year-old Indian girl, her long, black hair hangs loosely, momentarily hiding her innocent face.

                              TESS
          We have just witnessed the arrest of these two poachers.

Two middle-aged INDIAN MEN are pushed through the bush by an enthusiastic MOHAN, early 30s, a park employee.

They walk in the direction of a police vehicle.

                         TESS (CONT'D)
          Their story is similar to those of other poachers in Kenya,
          Tanzania, India, and Brazil. Men desperate for a quick fix, they
          track and kill these animals: for their tusks, claws, internal
          organs and, most importantly, the animals' skins.

Tess pulls the doors open on the panel truck.

TRUCK INTERIOR

Bloodied knives lie next to the dismembered bodies and pelts of two Bengal
tigers.

                                    TESS
              These skins and the body will pass through three or four middlemen
              finally being sold for forty thousand dollars on the black market
              in India and China.

Maya approaches from Tess's left. Tess motions for Dylan to follow her with the
camera.

Maya takes her finger and drags it along the blood stained floor of the truck.

Turning around, she takes her finger and marks a red dot in blood on Tess's
forehead.

EXT. ROADWAY FROM GAME PARK - LATER

Tess stares out from the open window of their vehicle as they head back toward
Mumbai.

Maya sits in the back seat next to Mohan.

                                    MOHAN
              Maybe we will have better luck tomorrow. Please come back with
              Maya and me for something to eat at my wife's restaurant.

                                    TESS
              Are you hungry?

Dylan nods yes and slides in a CD as they pass a bus terminal and parking lot
filled with waiting buses.

                                    DYLAN
              Endangered is a cluster fuck.

INT. HOTEL BAR - LATER THAT NIGHT

Tess sits at a corner table alone. Her only companion is a half empty bottle of
gin and a glass.

Tess eyes the bars inhabitants: couples, young women, hookers, businessmen.

Standing at the bar is someone who looks very familiar, JAMES GUARDIAN, early
50s, well-built, with a slightly receding hairline, talking with a very
attractive young, Asian woman, JULIET.

                                    TESS
              James Guardian

Tess pours gin into her empty glass. Tess quickly types his name into Google and waits. With one hand she clicks and reads with the other she fixes the strap on her bra so it his hidden, she seductively rises and heads toward the bar.

                         TESS (CONT'D)
          I think the gentleman would like a Cuervo with salt on the rim of
          the glass.

Guardian turns around, looks once then again.

                         JAMES
          You have an exceptional memory.

Juliet smiles, rubs James' thigh, turns and works her way into the crowd. As she mixes with the crowd, she passes and exchanges a glance with Dylan who, with one hand, drops some bills and removes a drink from a waiter's tray.

Dylan turns toward the bar and sees the connection that is being made with James and Tess.

Dylan sips from the drink turns and follows Juliet.

EXT. HARBOR WALKWAY - DESERTED TEMPLE - LATER THAT NIGHT

Tess and James walk along a man-made path toward the remains of a small abandoned temple.

                         JAMES
          There is retreat used by the English during their occupation. An
          old hotel and reserve where they could go hunt tigers and rhinos.
          I have been told that there are still a few tigers in hiding
          there.

                         TESS
          So, what is it that you are doing in Mumbai?

MONKEYS climb around a pink stone statue of entangled lovers.

                         JAMES
          I manage a company here.

                         TESS
          Overseas Placements? Domestics, au pairs, factory workers, an
          occasional cultural exchange...sounds like the flip side of the
          skin trade.

James looks at her like he is surprised at what she knows.

                         TESS (CONT'D)
          When I saw you earlier, I pulled you up on my iPad.

                         JAMES
          We refer to it as humanitarian intervention.

Tess turns back toward James, as a monkey swipes the cell phone clipped to her belt. Tess grabs at it, but the monkey is gone.

                              TESS
          The damn monkey stole my cell phone!

James takes a few steps in the direction of the primate thief.

                              JAMES
          Do you investigate all of the men that you...

                              TESS
          That I intend to sleep with? If my memory is correct... We did
          sleep together...

James walks toward what remains of a stone fountain. The same monkey screeches and climbs up into the trees. A light rain begins to fall.

He reaches out to kiss her. She hesitates for a moment.

                              JAMES
          No more who, what and where.

Tess flashes a flirtatious smile. They kiss.

INT. HOTEL ROOM - MUMBAI - FOLLOWING MORNING

Water from a barely-flowing shower lightly splashes down Tess's naked body as she sits, squatting on the smooth stone floor, littered with frangipani petals.

James sits, shirtless, in a wicker chair across from Tess's bed.

James flips through eight-by-ten photos taken at night along the red light district.

BATHROOM

Tess exits the bathroom, towel wrapped loosely around her torso.

Dropping the towel, she puts on a silk robe.

                              JAMES
          Falkland Road.

Seated on the bed, Tess pops open a bottle of pills, downing a couple with what is left of a bottle of vodka.

                              TESS
          Dylan and I took them the other night.

                              JAMES
          Who is Dylan?

                              TESS
          My cameraman. He was with me in Darfur.

Tess heads toward the window.

                              JAMES
          What about the tigers?

                              TESS
          From what I see, or don't see, they're already extinct. Let
          someone else care about the fucking tigers. You told me that
          you could help me get inside. Your company... You network with
          agencies, companies, and I'm sure some criminal organizations that
          relocate, and sell, many of these girls.

                              JAMES
          I don't sell. We only buy.

                              TESS
          Okay, your side of the bed is a little cleaner, but you must know
          some of the scumbags on the other side.

Tess turns and looks at him, as if wanting him and discarding him were
synonymous.

                              TESS (CONT'D)
          Let me get dressed and check my email.

James removes his jacket from a chair and walks toward Tess.

                              JAMES
          Breakfast?

                              TESS
          The guy from the game park. He and his wife have a small restaurant
          the back side of the hotel. Meet you there in forty-five minutes.

They embrace and kiss, businesslike, not passionately.

James smiles, touches her lips with his fingers. James turns and exits.

EXT. HOTEL RESTAURANT - MINUTES LATER

James sips an espresso and reads the *Herald Tribune*.

The chair across from him is pulled out and SAM FORD, late 40s, dark hair with a
two-day-old beard and sunglasses, sits down.

James folds the paper and places it to the side of the table.

                              JAMES
          And who are you?

                              SAM
          Sam Ford. I do not have a hell of a lot of time, so let's skip the
          pleasantries.

Sam reaches over and the two men shake hands.

                              JAMES
          What happened to David?

                              SAM
          The wife, the kids, quality time. You know how it is, he needed a
          break.

A WAITER approaches with a coffee and croissant already in hand.

                              SAM (CONT'D)
          Your mid-life crisis relationship with the Diane Sawyer-wannabe
          has got to stop.

                              JAMES
          They're now going to tell me who I can--

                              SAM
          Right. Who you can fuck. Is she that good? What bothers me and the
          boys back home is that this is obviously not about pussy. I mean,
          you're the king of pussy. The people you are dealing with don't
          need this kind of attention.

Sam eats the croissant and sips coffee almost simultaneously.

                              JAMES
          We went to school together. We had a brief relationship.

                              SAM
          I know. I don't care about the history or if she thinks you are
          Bono out there saving the fucking world.

                              JAMES
          Fine. Let's talk business, Keith Dalton is out of control.

                              SAM
          Your job is to keep the new self-crowned prince of the black
          market highway under control and most important interested. The
          most important thing right now is that he believes you're the guy
          with the money, the organization, and the connections.

Sam gulps the last sip of coffee.

                              JAMES
          Why don't we just skip all the fucking drama and go directly to
          the towelheads?

                                    SAM
          The contact here has decided to pay retail instead of wholesale.
          We are trying to find out how he made the connection, and who
          actually has the hardware.

CELL PHONE IMAGE

A female hand holds a cell phone that is pointed in the direction of James and
Sam.

James makes like he is ready to leave.

                                   JAMES
          Word is out that the Koreans are now involved. And it all could
          be bull-shit, we have seen nothing.

                                    SAM
          All you need to tell him is that an initial payment will be wired
          as soon as we know the merchandise is legit and available.

Sam looks out the window toward the center of Mumbai.

                                SAM (CONT'D)
          Your new girlfriend and her partner are excess baggage. We will
          get rid of them if you don't.

Sam puts on his sunglasses and leaves the café.

INT. HOTEL ROOM - MINUTES LATER LAPTOP

Tess clicks into her email. She scrolls through it: prescriptions for anti-
depressants, junk mail, *Newsweek* article and a photo of James standing alongside
a group of teenage girls with frozen smiles on all their faces.

Tess clicks to a close up of James. KNOCK on door.

The door closes behind Dylan. Tess clicks off her laptop.

                                  DYLAN
          You should really lock the door.

Dylan walks to a weathered bamboo chair and sits down.

                               DYLAN (CONT'D)
          Where were you last night?

                                  TESS
          Here, there. Why is it any of your fucking business?

Tess at the window, glances down to the street below.

                               TESS (CONT'D)
          Went out for an after-dinner drink.

                              DYLAN
          Back to the old medication?

EXT. STREET - CONTINUOUS

KEITH DALTON, a rough looking but attractive Englishman, and KIT, a pock-marked
Thai, late 30s, drive past in a black Range Rover.

INT. HOTEL ROOM - SAME

                              TESS
          Why in hell did I agree to do this?

Tess stops at the mirror.

                         TESS (CONT'D)
          Getting this assignment is like being some medium level
          politician in D.C. who is rewarded for a bad political move and
          being appointed the ambassador to Portugal. Not much happening in
          Portugal.

                              DYLAN
          Your problem has always been your desire to be on both sides of
          the line at the same time.

                              TESS
          Like having your cake and eating it, too? What good is the cake
          if you can't eat it?

Mirror reflection as she combs her wet hair.

Tess reaches for a bottle of scotch, knocking a half-filled glass onto the
floor.

The glass rolls in Dylan's direction, spilling liquor on photos scattered about
the floor.

                              DYLAN
          Have you spoken to your therapist?

Dylan picks a letter, the liquid runs off onto the floor.

                              TESS
          Please.

Tess pulls the paper from his hand.

                         TESS (CONT'D)
          When did we stop calling them psychiatrists or shrinks? Like
          going from crippled to handicapped and handicapped to physically-
          challenged. We change the nomenclature so that it makes people
          feel less victimized.

She picks up the bottle, swishes it teasingly at Dylan.

                         TESS (CONT'D)
     Feels like you can cut the air with a knife.

                         DYLAN
     Who is the guy you were with at the bar last night?

The silk robe falls to the floor. She's wearing nothing.

                         DYLAN (CONT'D)
Is this the cue for me to tell you what a great body you have for a woman your
age?

                         TESS
     Fuck you. I'm only 39.

                         DYLAN
You're 42 and put the robe back on. You didn't answer my question.

Picking up her robe, she puts it on.

                         TESS
     An old friend. Classmates at Columbia.

Dylan pauses as he opens the door.

                         TESS (CONT'D)
     I'm going across the street to have some breakfast with Mr.
     Guardian.

     Call me when you're ready to leave.

Tess stands a few feet away as Dylan exits her room.

                         DYLAN
     This is a pretty simple and safe assignment.

                         TESS
     The skin trade is a very nasty business.

INT. SMALL HOTEL RESTAURANT - KITCHEN - LATER

Maya stares at James who sits alone at a corner table.

LAKSHMI, a slight-looking INDIAN woman in her late 20s, and Mohan, in dress
shirt and slacks, are arguing with Keith, and Bihari in a police uniform, both
seen earlier in the Range Rover.

                         KEITH
     You were paid to do a very simple task.

                         BIHARI
     A Muslim married to Hindi trash.

Keith walks up to Mohan, their faces inches apart.

                                    KEITH
          Tomorrow, no more fucking excuses!

INT. RESTAURANT ENTRANCE - SAME

Maya hesitates as Tess enters the restaurant. TABLE

James pulls the upholstered chair away from the table so that Tess can sit down.
His attention turns back to the confrontation.

                                    BIHARI
          My boss been very kind to you. Why did you not do what you paid
          to do?

                                    MOHAN
          Because you lied to me.

Maya walks quietly toward Lakshmi.

                                    MAYA
          The reporter lady I told you about.

She points toward Tess, but Lakshmi's attention is elsewhere. Bihari motions to
Mohan to take this outside.

Keith exits, smiling at James as he leaves. Lakshmi and Maya both walk toward
Tess and James.

                                    LAKSHMI
          Welcome. So sorry. Some associates of my husband. Not so good
          with business.

Tess motions for Maya to be seated.

                                    LAKSHMI (CONT'D)
          Maya told me about the dead tigers.

EXT. STREET IN FRONT OF RESTAURANT - CONTINUOUS

Bihari and Keith continue to threaten Mohan.

                                    BIHARI
          The only reason you are still alive is because of me. You have
          family in Pakistan who are very disappointed.

Keith turns and looks at Maya.

                                    KEITH
          You have a very beautiful daughter.

INT. RESTAURANT - TABLE

Lakshmi places tea and biscuits onto the table.

James examines an Air India poster--a blurred, out-of-focus photo of a tiger disappearing into the tropical forest--taped next to it is a poster of Bin Laden.

                         JAMES
          I'm not sure what you're looking for.

                         TESS
          What I'm looking for?

                         JAMES
          It's just hard to believe that someone with your background is--

                         TESS
          My background?

                         JAMES
          Well, after your nightly coverage of 9/11, you were in and out of
          Afghanistan, Pakistan and Iraq.

          Prior to that, you were the only female correspondent who was
          allowed to interview Kim Jong.

          Not exactly the second-tier circuit. After the incident in Darfur,
          you vanished.

                         TESS
          I'm back. Looking for tigers that I cannot find. The wardens,
          animal-rights activists claim they can hear them, smell them. I
          would just like to see one, face-to-face.

James motions for Maya to move closer to Tess. Tess reaches out and takes hold of James's hand.

                         TESS (CONT'D)
          If you know so much about me, you also know that after Darfur I
          had to... to take some time off.

                         JAMES
          I read the papers.

                         TESS
          I don't.

In a faded mirror, Tess sees the reflection of Dylan pausing a moment, gawking at two young women who pass the restaurant.

Tess takes a sip of tea, while Maya stands fixated on James.

A large, rugged hand, with a silver ring spelling Baghdad, rests on Tess's shoulder.

She tilts her head back as Dylan's other hand caresses her other shoulder. A
weathered Yankees cap fits snugly above his furrowed face as he kisses Tess on
the forehead.

                              DYLAN
          I see you're feeling better.

                              TESS
          Dylan, No. This is...

Tess motions with her eyes for Dylan to sit.

She smiles seductively at James and then turns to Dylan.

                         TESS (CONT'D)
          Dylan, this is my old friend, James, James Guardian. Dylan
          Jennings, DP extraordinaire.

                              JAMES
          Good morning.

Dylan continues to stare at James suspiciously. James rises from his chair,
intending to shake hands.

Dylan nods with a late response.

                              TESS
          Have you spoken with Mohan?

                              DYLAN
          Going back later this afternoon.

                              JAMES
          Maybe you should hire the poachers as your guides.

                              DYLAN
          Splendid idea, James. What is it that you do here in--

                              JAMES
          Business, sourcing abroad.

Dylan takes off his Yankee cap, placing it on Maya's head.

                              DYLAN
          Oh yes, sourcing abroad, putting the Pacific Rim on the map. In
          ten years, the way things are going, business men like you will
          have turned the U.S. into a third-world economy.

Tess ignores his sarcasm.

                              JAMES
          I'm sorry, but I don't think I fit your Michael Moore-stereotype
          and what I do is really none of your business.

Dylan looks into the cup to see what Tess is drinking, while James pays for Tess's tab.

                              JAMES (CONT'D)
          How much longer are you going to be in India?

James looks at Tess.

                              DYLAN
          I'm on assignment. Who knows?

                              JAMES
          There is a party at the British Consulate on Saturday.

James writes the address on a paper napkin and slides it to Tess. Tess smiles seductively.

                              TESS
          I'll take a look at our... at my schedule.

James rises and places a few bills on the table.

                              JAMES
          I'll pick you up at eight o'clock.

Dylan slides into James's seat and eats the remaining biscuit from his plate.

Tess gathers her belongings.

From the window, Dylan watches James enter his Audi, staring hard at the side panel: "Overseas Placements" with an image of a smiling girl's face. The car pulls away.

                              TESS
          He knows the city, pays for dinner, and I like the way he puts me
          to bed at night.

EXT. PARKING LOT - BENGAL HOTEL - MOMENTS LATER

Dylan motions to Tess, directing her to the front of the car. Tess climbs into passenger side of the Jeep.

                              TESS
          Men. Aren't you a bit old for that whose-dick-is-bigger bullshit?

                              DYLAN
          He looks like the kind of guy who will ask you to use mouthwash
          before you give him a blowjob.

                              TESS
          Hasn't happened yet.

Dylan is silent as the vehicle turns out onto the highway.

INT. MAYA'S CLOSET-SIZED BEDROOM - SAME

Maya, now seated on her bed, opens a weathered photo album. FLASHBACK

SUPER - EXT. ROADWAY SOUTHERN INDIA - A FEW MONTHS AGO - AFTERNOON

A weathered passenger bus travels along a rural semitropical highway. Windows, blurred with dust, partially conceal the bus passengers, twenty teenage Asian girls.

INT. BUS - SAME

The bus driver, a disheveled Asian man, MOOKIE, late 30s, acne-scarred skin, looks into the rear view mirror.

Empty water bottles, food wrappings and spoiled fruit litter the rusted floor of the bus.

The girls, dressed in hand-me-downs or throwaway clothes, carry few possessions. A few sleep, others stare hopelessly out the filthy windows.

Maya sits with her long, black hair loosely hanging, momentarily hiding her innocent face and deep blue eyes.

Maya opens her knapsack, gingerly pulling out a small tattered photo album.

The Thai girl sitting next to her,11- or 12-years-old, speaks in a slow whisper.

                         GIRL
          I was coming home from school with a friend. We were on the high
          road.

Maya looks at the young girl for a moment, then turns and stares hauntingly out the window.

                         MAYA
          I was with my mother and younger brother. He could not hold on.
          She tried to save him.

Maya carefully turns the water-damaged pages.

                         GIRL
          Where is this ugly man taking us?

                         MAYA
          We are going to Mumbai. Do you have family there?

The young girl shrugs her shoulders and shakes her head no.

EXT. ROADSIDE - CONTINUOUS

A patchwork of urban decay pockmarked by random tropical landscapes.

INT. BUS - SAME

Mookie's cell phone RINGS.

                              MOOKIE
                          (in Indonesian)
        Ya. Fuck you. What do I have? The usual, a bus load, minus one.
        She was sick. Left her with a border guard. The dickhead gave
        me one hundred and fifty dollars... covers expenses. How old?
        Maybe 11, 12... Blow me... I should arrive in four days... Got you
        covered man... Where? Great... Ya, I know the roads... How much?
        Bihari! How much? Where the fuck did you go? Bihari, you dot-head
        motherfucker!

The cell phone goes dead. Mookie glances at the rear view mirror.

Maya stares at him with a look that could kill. Through the reflection in the
mirror, he puckers and blows her a kiss.

INT. REAR OF BUS - MOMENTS LATER

Tears streak the face of the young girl seated next to Maya.

Maya carefully thumbs through the album. She stops to examine a photo of three
girls standing knee-deep in ocean surf on a good day.

BACK TO PRESENT

SUPER -- INT. MAYA'S BEDROOM

Maya covers her face with her hand, trying to privately remember this simple, but
precious, moment.

INT. EDITING ROOM - MUMBAI - LATER

Dylan and Tess watch the monitor: footage of poachers being arrested and led out
of the jungle foliage, dark blotches cloud the screen. Dylan fiddles with the
controls.

                              DYLAN
        Shit!

Tess stares blankly at the monitor.

                          DYLAN (CONT'D)
        Passé. In a few years, we will be able to clone anything we want.

Dylan glares at Tess.

                              TESS
        Great. We have to arrest these two assholes and where do we get
        the new dead tigers?

Tess turns and heads for the door.

                              TESS (CONT'D)
        Fuck you and the tigers!

INT. EDITING ROOM - FOLLOWING MORNING

Dylan is sleeping in a chair. Eleven o'clock, the ventilator slats RATTLE. Remi, enters the room and, as usual, slams the door.

Dylan opens his eyes.

                              DYLAN
        Have you heard from Tess?

                              REMI
        She's not answering. I'm packing up. I'll meet you downstairs.

Remi packs up the equipment and exits. Dylan walks over to the computer, checking his email, then clicks on NEW

Dylan gets up and walks to the large pair of windows. A storm rages outside.

Remi sits in the Jeep downstairs, beeping the horn.

Dylan picks up his bag from the table and heads toward his SECRETARY.

                              SECRETARY
        Things have changed. They want you to head out to Rajgarh to
        cover the aftermath of the storm. Remi is waiting for you
        downstairs.

                              DYLAN
If Ms. Douglas calls, tell her we need to talk.

INT. TESS'S HOTEL BEDROOM - 2:00 AM

Tess rises abruptly from her sleep. Tess reaches for the empty bottle of vodka on the side table and gets up and looks at the clock. She sees her naked reflection in the mirror and throws the empty bottle, smashing the mirror.

                              TESS
        When are they going to leave me alone!

She puts on her silk robe and staggers out onto the terrace.

EXT. MAIN STREET - MOMENTS LATER

Jeep pulls to a sudden stop at a red light. Dylan gets out, turns, and gives Remi the finger as the vehicle SCREECHES and pulls away.

Dylan and Tess exchange a glance.

INT. TESS'S ROOM - MINUTES LATER

Tess staggers across the room, knocking over a chair and ripping clothes from the closet door.

                              TESS
          Leave me the fuck alone! They said you told them not to bring me
          any... Who the fuck do you think you are?

Dylan tries to move her toward the bed.

                              TESS (CONT'D)
          You want to have sex with me again? Let's split a bottle of vodka.

She falls onto the bed. She pulls herself against the bed covers and starts sobbing.

                              TESS (CONT'D)
          You didn't take us to that place, I did.

He gently strokes her back and shoulders.

                              DYLAN
          I'll stay here until you go to sleep.

                              TESS
          It has to stop. I can't sleep.

                              DYLAN
          You were an observer, not a participant.

Tess attempts to smile to stop herself from crying.

                              TESS
          That's bullshit. We both know what happened! We fucked up. We
          should have not been there!

She pulls the sheet over her body.

                              TESS (CONT'D)
          Most nights it's as if it's on film, a movie, not a dry eye in
          the house. Fucking Academy Award material! Kidman, Roberts, Jolie
          could really pull it off.

She freezes for a moment as their eyes meet.

                              TESS (CONT'D)
          You act like you weren't even there.

                              DYLAN
          No one in this business gets to be 40 without some cuts and
          bruises. We tell the news. And most of the time the news is bad.

                              TESS
          Cuts and bruises... Fuck you! Zoloft, Paxil and Wellbutrin...

Tess picks up an empty bottle of scotch.

                           TESS (CONT'D)
          And this shit is the only thing that...

There is a KNOCK at the door.

A YOUNG WAITER enters the room carrying a tray with coffee and biscuits.

The waiter puts it on the table and leaves.

                              DYLAN
               Drink it!

Reluctantly, she takes a sip.

                              TESS
               Do you ever ask yourself why they didn't kill us?

                              DYLAN
               We got lucky.

Tess takes Dylan's hand and places it on her breast over her heart.

                              TESS
               Just one drink...

Dylan strokes her shoulder as she kisses him.

Resting against the additional pillow she closes her eyes. FLASHBACK

EXT. HYDRA, DARFUR - DESOLATE STREET - AFTERNOON

Dylan closes the door of the jeep, adjusts the video camera to his shoulder and
follows a younger Tess, down a war-torn village street.

                              DYLAN
               These guys look just like the guys we are supposed to running
               from.

An empty battered white bus passes.

                              TESS
               They claim the women and children were relocated. Bullshit!

Tess walks toward a battered schoolhouse. A GOVERNMENT SOLDIER, approaches with
his hand flagging in the air.

                              SOLDIER
               Your fifteen minutes are up.

Tess adjusts her headset as her cell phone RINGS.

                              TESS
          Shit... We are live in five minutes!

                             SOLDIER
          This is what you wanted to see. You must leave. I don't give a
          flying fuck if Larry King is on the other end of that...

Tess answers the phone.

                           PHONE (V.O.)
          Tess, this is David. Can you hear me? Are you ready?

Tess fools with her headset.

                              TESS
          Hello? Hello? Why don't these fucking things ever work?

Tess walks forward, tossing the phone to Dylan.

                             DYLAN
                           (TO Tess)
          Good or bad, these guys do not fuck around.

                             SOLDIER
          Am I speaking fucking English?

Perimeter EXPLOSIONS drown out the soldier's diatribe.

                              TESS
          Let's go with what we've got.

They both move closer.

                          TESS (CONT'D)
          This is all that remains of the town of Hydra, in western Darfur.
          Where are the women and children?

SOLDIERS surround the burned and bombed out stone buildings. Tess and Dylan walk
toward one of the buildings.

                         SOLDIER'S VOICE
          They ran away to... They were taken to a refugee camp!

                              TESS
          So they can be raped and mutilated, and their children drugged
          and sent off to kill their own family and friends.

The man points with his rifle at Dylan and then at Tess.

INT. SCHOOL HOUSE - EMPTY

GODIE, a 13-year-old male civilian, medium height, thin, wearing a ragged
Madonna T-shirt, carrying a rifle over his shoulder, walks toward Tess and
Dylan. A SOLDIER shoves Godie back.

EXT. FRONT OF SCHOOLHOUSE

EXPLODING SHELLS, GUN FIRE. Tess and Dylan hurriedly leave the building. Godie
blocks their path.

                         GODIE (SOFTLY IN BROKEN ENGLISH)
          My name, Godie. These men are all liars. They are farmers that
          have been given guns. They work for the government. They have
          raped and stolen all of the women of this village. They took my
          mother and killed my father.

Godie and Tess stand fixated on each other as two soldiers approach.

                         SOLDIER
          Move it! Get the fuck out of here.

Godie is pushed away by two soldiers as he grabs Tess's arm.

                         SOLDIER (CONT'D)
          Get her the hell out of here!

Another soldier grabs him from behind, spins him around and jabs the rifle butt
in his back.

                         GODIE
          I know where they have them.

Tess feels something in Godie's hand as Godie is escorted away.

                         GODIE (CONT'D)
          The foreigners.

In the distance a number of armed men on camels approach.

Tess and Dylan begin to walk and then run toward the army vehicle that they
arrived in.

                         DYLAN
          The evil men on horseback, camel-back are... I suggest we pack up
          and get the hell out of here!

Tess pauses and takes a deep breath.

                         GODIE
          If I show you... If I take you where they are... I come with you.
          You take me with you when you leave?

Godie walks around them as the soldiers he came in with begin to set fire to the
remaining buildings.

                         GODIE (CONT'D)
          You looking for the Dutch girls?

                              TESS
          I thought they were.

                              DYLAN
          They're dead.

Exploding SHELLS. Tess turns around and watches as Godie walks toward one of the
pickup trucks.

                              DYLAN (CONT'D)
          Where the fuck is the driver?

The pickup truck, with Godie driving, circles them then stops.

                              GODIE
          You want story or you going to stay here and watch buildings
          burn? He get tired of looking at you he shoot you dead.

Dylan focuses the camera on Tess as Godie accelerates causing the wind to push
her hair back, revealing her sculptured face.

                              DYLAN
          Where the hell are we going?

Godie smiles as Dylan focuses his camera on him.

                              GODIE
          You want a real story, get in the fucking truck.

SUPER - BACK TO INT. MUMBAI HOTEL ROOM - HOURS LATER

The moonlight filters through the blinds. Tess pulls herself up, resting her
head against the backboard.

Dylan sits in a chair facing the balcony of the room.

Tess glances across the room toward Dylan, who sits alone in a wicker chair in
front of the window. She empties her bag onto the bed looking for her pills.

                              TESS
          James invited me to go away with him.

                              DYLAN
          The alcohol clearly hasn't altered your choice in men.

Tess slides out of bed and heads across the room, past Dylan, through the French
doors and onto the veranda.

                              TESS
          Some place in the hills. He says he knows where we, where one can
          find...

                              DYLAN
          I take it I'm not invited.

                                    TESS
          This is the first man that I have had a relationship in over a year.

                                    DYLAN
          What would you call what we had?

Tess turns and stares at Dylan with a frustrated smile.

                                    TESS
          Road sex. It happens all the time.

Tess sees Dylan's sullen expression.

                                    TESS (CONT'D)
          I'm sorry. It was a lovely intimate moment... or moments. But I
          thought we had both gotten over it.

Tess heads into the bathroom and closes the door. Dylan puts the photos in his
bag and exits.

INT. TESS'S ROOM - MOMENTS LATER

Tess dials a number on her cell phone while she looks at a number of photos
sitting on her dresser.

INT. AIRPORT GATE - SAME

James answers his cell phone.

                                    JAMES
          What do you mean he has changed his mind? I thought you already
          went over this with him?

A number of young girls sit waiting to board an airplane.

SPLIT SCREEN

                                    JAMES
          Find out how much he wants.

                                    KEITH
          He says it's not about the money.

BOARDING GATE

James stares at the girls as they board the plane.

                                    KEITH
          It seems he suddenly has a fucking conscience.

                                    JAMES
          A fucking Muslim with a conscience! It's not going to do him any
          good if he's a dead man. CLICK

A YOUNG FEMALE ATTENDANT approaches. James removes the tickets from his coat
pocket. The attendant looks at the girls then questionably at James.

                         JAMES (to the attendant) (CONT'D)
          A soccer team.

The attendant nods and smiles.

The attendant turns and walks back toward the boarding area.

INT. INDIAN RESTAURANT - NEXT DAY

Lakshmi heads toward the restaurant office. There is some NOISE coming from the
back of the restaurant. Lakshmi enters the back room to find Mohan waving a
knife in the air as Maya hides behind him.

                              KEITH
          Take the girl!

Keith LAUGHS as Bihari grabs hold of Maya.

                              LAKSHMI
          Maya! Let go of her!

                              KEITH
          We made a deal and you...

                              MOHAN
          I was told it was only to be used as a ransom!

Mohan tries to hit Keith but misses. Bihari laughs as Maya fights to free
herself.

                              BIHARI
          You betrayed your Muslim brothers.

                              MOHAN
                         (to Lakshmi)
          I have told them everything I know!

EXT. BENGAL HOTEL - PARKING AREA

Dylan exits the Jeep and walks toward the restaurant.

INT. RESTAURANT - SAME

Mohan lunges at Bihari, slashing him across the cheek with a knife.

                              KEITH
          What the fuck are you waiting for?

Keith SHOOTS Mohan.

                                    LAKSHMI
                                  (screaming)
          No!

Keith steps closer and fires two more shots into Mohan's chest. Lakshmi attacks
Bihari, but is knocked away, hitting the wall.

Bleeding from the mouth and nose, she collapses to the floor.

                                    KEITH
          Get rid of both of them.

INT. RESTAURANT - CONTINUOUS

Dylan enters the restaurant. Mohan lies dead on the floor. Lakshmi stands
sobbing over him. Keith stands behind her with the gun pointed at her head.

Keith turns with the gun pointed at Dylan. Bihari grabs Maya and heads toward
the door.

                                    DYLAN
          What the hell is going on?!

                                    LAKSHMI
          They kill my husband. He told them what they wanted, and they
          kill him anyway!

Dylan takes a few steps toward Bihari and Maya.

                                    DYLAN
          Put the girl down!

                                    KEITH
          Billy Bob. I don't think this is the time to play hero. The girl
          is just a little dessert after the main course.

                                    BIHARI
          The girl does not belong to them. We are both with the police
          department.

Bihari passes with Maya in tow.

                                    KEITH
          They broke the law. This is not their daughter, and he tried to
          kill a police Officer.

EXT. RESTAURANT - CONTINUOUS

A CROWD has begun to assemble in front of the restaurant. Keith turns and lowers
the gun.

INT. RESTAURANT - CONTINUOUS

                              KEITH
          You are interfering in police business.

                              DYLAN
          And since when are you with the police?

                              KEITH
          Since I have a gun pointed at your fucking head.

EXT. STREET OUTSIDE - RESTAURANT

Keith slowly backs out of the restaurant toward the open van door. Bihari opens
the passenger door and shoves Maya inside.

Keith climbs in behind the wheel, gun still in hand. The van pulls away.

Locals console Lakshmi. A police SIREN is heard. Dylan exits the restaurant.

                              DYLAN
          Do you want me to take you to the police?

                              LAKSHMI
          She not my sister like I said, but this not about the girl. My
          husband know some very bad people.

                              DYLAN
          Is he working with the poachers?

Lakshmi looks confused and shakes her head no.

                              LAKSHMI
          He told me he was going to be paid much money for information he
          had, but he change his mind.

INT. RESTAURANT - CONTINUOUS

Dylan examines Mohan's body, the kitchen knife still clutched in his hand.

                              DYLAN
          He's dead.

Two older women try to pull Lakshmi away. One of the women whispers to her in
Hindi.

                              LAKSHMI
          I have to leave... Go away.

A number of the women escort Lakshmi down a side avenue. Dylan heads back toward
his Jeep.

INT. ALLURE GUEST HOUSE - TESS'S ROOM - LATE AFTERNOON

A knock on the door. The door opens and Dylan enters and slowly walks through an
empty room.

Dylan turns on Tess's computer and tries to check her email but the password does not work. Dylan remembers the conversation with Tess, and then types in "tiger lady."

Quick scroll through.

Three days after being interviewed about the skin trade by *Time*, the older of the two girls was found murdered.

Overseas Placements Ltd. was mentioned five times. James Guardian was interviewed for the article. He had brought the girls into the country ten months ago from Uzbekistan to work as nannies. Somehow they ended up dead in a brothel in Miami.

Second page: a photo of a dead girl, feet and hands bound, throat slit, mutilated.

> DYLAN
> (reading)
> Mustang Motel, Miami. 'Angel' (stage name) had been dead for three days. They found her diary, most of it ripped away... included a drawing from one of the pages.

Dylan clicks on the drawing. A skeleton-like figure curled up in a small ball-like shape on a bed. A number of stick-men with erections circle the bed.

> DYLAN (CONT'D)
> The notebook had an Overseas Placements sticker on the first page. The murder investigation went south, nothing. Our real endangered species are walking up right on two legs.

EXT. MANGO TREE - EARLY EVENING

The monkey sits with the cell phone high in the tree tops. Another monkey next to him eats a mango. The monkey bites on the cell phone.

The monkey pushes some of the buttons and a picture of Tess and her sister appears. Another click, a picture of James. The phone RINGS. The monkey is startled and the phone falls through the tree branches to the ground. The phone lands, open-faced, a picture of James and Sam at the café.

INT. BRITISH CONSULATE - LATER THAT EVENING

Consulate party. EXPATRIATES dressed in ivory linen suits, INDIAN MEN in hand-tailored business ones, a racial mixture of all ages.

Tess walks through the crowd carrying two drinks as she approaches James, who is talking with the very lovely, mid-20s, Chinese female named, JULIET. Seen earlier at the hotel bar.

> JULIET
> So, you finally stopped chasing the elusive tiger and made it back to Mumbai?

                              TESS
          I'm a New Yorker, much more at home in the urban jungle.

Dylan, casually dressed, his face scratched and bruised.

                             DYLAN
          Tess!

James and Dylan glare at each other intensely.

                         DYLAN (CONT'D)
          Good evening, Mr. Guardian.

Dylan downs his drink.

                         DYLAN (CONT'D)
          I went to police headquarters. No one knows anything about the
          girl or the murder.

                              TESS
          What?

                             JAMES
          This is India, these things happen everyday.

                              TESS
          James is going to talk with the police.

Dylan stares at Tess.

                             DYLAN
          I have been trying to get you all day.

                              TESS
          I lost my cell a few days ago. Well, it was actually--

                             DYLAN
          We have a shoot to finish tomorrow.

Tess turns and smiles at James and steps towards Dylan, separating the two of them.

                         DYLAN (CONT'D)
          I get the feeling there is going to be a rather dramatic change
          in our, in your story line. I saw your email. It's over, this is
          not another--

                              TESS
          We will talk later. Good night.

Tess takes a drink from a waiter's tray as she and James turn and walk away.

                            TESS (CONT'D)
          I... I would like to apologize. He sometimes has the habit of
          being an asshole.

                            JAMES
          Would you like something to eat?

An older gentleman with a clergyman's collar, REV. HIGGENS, stops, smiles, and
politely interrupts the conversation.

                            HIGGENS
          Excuse me, James. I just wanted to thank you again for what you
          are doing for so many of our children. We just received three
          letters this week thanking us.

                            JAMES
          Rev. Higgens, this is Ms. Douglas, a correspondent from the States.

                            HIGGENS
          Very nice to meet you. I don't want to take up any more of your
          time.

                            JAMES
          I will talk to you later in the week.

James takes Tess by the arm and leads her to the dining area. Tess watches
Juliet.

                            TESS
          That is the same woman I saw you talking to the other night at
          the hotel bar?

                            JAMES
          A business acquaintance.

Juliet, from a short distance, smiles. Tess pauses and turns toward James.

                            TESS
          Maya, the girl from the restaurant?

                            JAMES
          She was a refugee from one of the coastal villages, decimated by
          the wave.

                            TESS
          Yesterday the police... There was an altercation at the restaurant
          and her father was killed.

                            JAMES
          He was not her father. That was the man her sister was living
          with. Her sister left China six or seven years ago. He was under
          investigation. Word was out that he has family connections to the
          Taliban.

                                  TESS
          Don't half the Muslims on the planet have a family connection to
          the--

                                  JAMES
          Look, in the morning I will contact the police and find out where
          the girl was taken.

Tess smiles as she drinks the remainder of her cocktail. James walks away toward
an open veranda, Tess follows. Mumbai rests mysteriously against the night sky.

INT. BAR AREA - CONTINUOUS

Dylan stands at the bar alongside an old acquaintance, MIC CHESTERFIELD, a BBC
correspondent, with short cropped hair, a two day-old beard, in his mid-40s. He
seems to be downing a tray-load of martinis.

                                  CHESTERFIELD
          It has been a while. I didn't see you after the embassy bombing.

                                  DYLAN
          Guess you didn't know where to look. I hung around for a few days,
          and then they sent me to Indonesia two days after the fucking
          tsunami. I'm now working here in lovely Mumbai.

Chesterfield flirts with a young waitress.

                                  CHESTERFIELD
          Aren't these women fucking amazing?

                                  DYLAN
          I haven't noticed.

                                  CHESTERFIELD
          The blue-black hair, the dark lips, nipples like black olives,
          pink pussy against the dark thighs.

Chesterfield steers Dylan toward the beautiful Juliet.

                                  DYLAN
          From what I remember, you would fuck a snake if it lay still long
          enough. Who is she?

                                  CHESTERFIELD
          Eat shit and die...

Chesterfield downs another drink.

                                  CHESTERFIELD (CONT'D)
          She runs the most expensive massage parlor. I'm sorry, health
          club, in Mumbai, the very best.

Dylan continues to stare at her.

                         CHESTERFIELD (CONT'D)
          A 14-year old virgin will sit on your face for fifty pounds...
          spotless, guaranteed free of HIV. The ex-Pats refer to her as Mumbai
          Heidi.

Dylan looks back at James and Tess, who are engaged in a very intimate
conversation.

                         DYLAN
          There ought to be a law against people looking that good.

                         CHESTERFIELD
          Guardian and I share a cigar and occasionally a game of chess.

Dylan takes another drink.

                         CHESTERFIELD (CONT'D)
          He does some charity work with orphaned and abandoned teens --
          finds them jobs, families, nannies. There are rumors that he
          also works the highway.

                         DYLAN
          Highway?

                         CHESTERFIELD
          The dark road of black market commerce.

Chesterfield watches Dylan, who watches Juliet work her way through the crowd.
Dylan downs another drink.

                         DYLAN
          Juliet looks like she could...

                         CHESTERFIELD
          Juliet can get you anything you want.

Chesterfield looks at Dylan with a curious smile.

                         CHESTERFIELD (CONT'D)
          Tantra Palace, two blocks east of the Oberoi. Ask any cab driver.

Chesterfield looks at James and Tess again, and raises his glass in a mock
salute.

                         CHESTERFIELD (CONT'D)
          It may be time to castle James.

EXT. MOTEL - THAT NIGHT

A run down motel rests along a length of urban decay.

MOTEL ROOM

Tacky interior of a small room. A mixed group of ten to twelve adolescent GIRLS.
Some sit or lie on the floor. A few, looking exhausted, stretch out on a soiled
bed.

INDIAN GIRL sits in a wicker chair, combing a YOUNGER GIRL'S hair.

                         YOUNGER GIRL
         Where are they going to take us?

                         GIRL WITH COMB
         Somewhere to work.

Seated in the corner is an OLDER NEPALESE GIRL, perhaps 17, who gets up and
walks toward a gated steel window.

Maya exits the bathroom. Her long, black hair hangs loosely, momentarily hiding
her innocent face and deep-blue eyes.

                         NEPALESE GIRL
         I'm going to London to take care of children.

                         MAYA
         Oh, yes. And you will make money to send back to your family.

                         NEPALESE GIRL
         You make it sound like they tell us lies.

The door opens and a WESTERN MAN, early 50s and overweight, enters, followed by
Bihari, who looks over the room as if it is empty. Bihari takes some bills from
the man, points to a pole and curtain pulled half-way open revealing a single
bed, turns and exits slamming the door behind him.

The man scans the room, stepping awkwardly toward the young girl who was having
her hair combed.

                         WESTERN MAN
         How old are you?

She does not understand. Taking hold of her arm, he pulls her away from the bed.

                         MAYA
         No English. She is sick, wrong time of the month.

The man turns as Maya walks behind the man to the side of the bed. Taking her
hand, she gently pushes the girl back down on the bed.

                         MAYA (HINDI) (CONT'D)
         Do not worry. No one will hurt you.

Maya steps forward, unbuttoning her shirt, exposing her torso to the man.

                         MAYA (CONT'D)
         I am young, only 14. I'm what you want.

Maya turns and walks toward the curtained chamber. The man stands motionless for a moment.

The young girl on the bed looks at him with fear and disgust. The man pulls the curtain closed.

                         GIRL WITH COMB
                            (Hindi)
          I wish the water would have taken me.

Soft CRIES, MOANS, and heavy BREATHING are heard from the other room. The MUSIC increases in volume.

The curtain suddenly pulls open. The man exits, stuffing his shirt into his pants. Not looking at any of the other girls, he pulls up his zipper and exits the room.

Maya walks slowly through the curtain, past the girls and into the small bathroom.

The bathroom door remains open. Maya falls to her knees in front of the toilet, gagging herself, trying to regurgitate.

INT. VICTORIAN BUILDING HOUSING - CHILD WELFARE OFFICE AND ORPHANAGE - SUBURBS - NEXT DAY

James stands in the middle of a hallway surrounded by CHILDREN as Tess stands to his left talking with a young NUN.

                            NUN
          What Mr. Guardian has done for these children!

The minister seen at the party approaches.

                         NUN (CONT'D)
          He has been a godsend!

Tess continues to watch as James talks with three of the older FEMALE CHILDREN.

                         NUN (CONT'D)
          Beaten by her father and left out on the road to die. She has
          been here for almost six years.

Tess walks toward James, who is now watching a group of BOYS play soccer.

                            TESS
          I guess my questions have been answered.

                            NUN
          I'm sorry. What did you say?

                              TESS
          Nothing, talking to myself.

INT. DYLAN'S HOTEL ROOM - SAME

Dylan rummages through one of his aluminum camera cases. Inside is a
disassembled army revolver. He pieces it together, assembles a full clip and
carefully slides it in.

Engraved on the handle is "From Baghdad with Love." He gently removes the clip,
puts it in his pocket and stuffs the gun into the back of his pants.

EXT. MUMBAI NEIGHBORHOOD MARKET - AFTERNOON

Tess and James playfully roam through the stands and booths. Tess buys a cell
phone to replace the one stolen by the monkey.

An OLD SIKH wearing a white turban sits on a clean yellow cloth. Beside him
sits a pretty 6-year-old GIRL. Tess is drawn to her. The old man hears their
footsteps.

                         OLD SIKH
          You want to know what is in your future? I give you very good
          future. Five rupees.

                         JAMES
          I'll give you one rupee for both of us.

                         OLD SIKH
          As you like, sir. But if you want good future...

Tess hands the girl some money. She counts and in a LOW VOICE tells the old man
how much it is. He seems pleased.

                         OLD SIKH (CONT'D)
          Sir, you shall be first.

The old man picks up a deck of hand-painted fortune cards and spreads them on
the cloth in front of him, face down.

The little girl closes her eyes, pulls out one of the cards and WHISPERS
something as she hands it over to the old man.

On the card is a picture of Kali, a naked goddess with a garland of blood-
dripping skulls. The old man straightens his back and exclaims.

                         OLD SIKH (CONT'D)
          You, sir, must bow to a higher power. You will bow to her or like
          the mighty tiger, she will stalk you and drink your blood.

Tess smiles as the young girl lets her hand hover over the cards for a while.
Taking a long time to decide, she then resolutely picks the last card, which has
the image of the goddess Durga, riding a tiger.

                              OLD SIKH (CONT'D)
You shall struggle hard, but you shall overcome!

                                   TESS
What does the picture mean?

                              YOUNG GIRL
Very important. Durga is riding a tiger. All of us fight with the
tiger inside. When we have mastered the tiger, we have learned to
be our own master, to balance the good and the evil, when one has
connected with the spirit within, it is "breaking the tiger."

                                   TESS
                         (pensively) Thank you.
Tess drops a number of rupees at the young girl's feet and
follows James through the crowded street.

INT. JAMES'S BEDROOM - SAME NIGHT

James is asleep. Tess turns over and picks up the cell phone.

                                   TESS

Yes. Room 521.

The phone RINGS a number of times as Tess looks at a photo of James, Juliet and
a group of young girls. The girls are waving goodbye.

                              VOICE ON PHONE
I'm sorry but Mr. Jennings is not in.

                                   TESS
Thank you. When he does come back would you tell him to give me a
call? Thank you.

Tess lies back as James moves across the bed and pulls her into his arms.

                                   JAMES
I am sure your Mr. Jennings is in good hands.

EXT. TANTRA PALACE - LATER

Dylan parks his Jeep, gets out and enters the building.

INT. TANTRA PALACE - MOMENTS LATER

Juliet steps out from behind a red satin drape and greets him with a formal bow
and hands pressed together, as if to say "namaste" (I greet the god within you).

                                  JULIET
Come this way, please. (To the receptionist)

Deepa, tell Ramaji we have a guest.

Juliet leads him into a grandiose office.

A large pink stone statue of two lovers sits like a prop on the floor behind
her.

                         JULIET (CONT'D)
          Now, what can we do for you?

                              DYLAN
          We have a mutual friend.

                              JULIET
          You do look familiar. Oh yes, you're a friend of the woman that
          James is...

Dylan examines the room as he takes a seat across from Juliet.

                         JULIET (CONT'D)
          The news correspondent and you are her cameraman. Endangered
          species.

Dylan does not seem to be amused. Juliet walks to a large pair of French windows
that look out onto a market area of Mumbai.

                         JULIET (CONT'D)
          So what can I help you with?

                              DYLAN
          A 14-year-old girl?

                              JULIET
          What makes you think I would be able to help you with a... We
          don't deal with children.

                              DYLAN
          It's pretty well known around town that you help men with their
          special needs.

                              JULIET
          Is that so? I didn't know we were listed in the tourist guide. I
          am very sorry but I cannot help you.

Dylan pulls the chair close to her, making it difficult for her to leave.

                              DYLAN
                         (sarcastic)
          But, I've heard so much about Indian hospitality.

Dylan's hand moves slowly down her body stopping at her exposed knee.

                         DYLAN (CONT'D)
          You're in the flesh business.

Juliet reaches over and runs her hand across his stomach and groin.

                              JULIET
          I am in the entertainment business.

Juliet takes his hand and moves it up her skirt.

                              DYLAN
          Mumbai Heidi. Isn't that what they call you?

Juliet moves her hand to his waist and around his back, to his pistol stuck in
the waistband of his pants.

Dylan pushes her hand off and removes the gun, pressing it against her bare
belly.

                              JULIET
          You're hurting me!

                              DYLAN
          Right now, I don't give a shit how many girls you have bought or
          sold. I just want one of them. A 14-year-old named Maya.

Juliet tries to push him away, knocking his baseball cap off. Dylan pushes her
back down, ripping her sari.

                              JULIET
          Look, I have a lovely woman for you, two of them if you like on
          the house.

Dylan presses the gun firmly against her chest.

                              JULIET (CONT'D)
          You were in Baghdad?

                              DYLAN
          Bush One and Bush Two. Let's cut to the chase. Baghdad déjà vu.

Helpless woman being questioned by a hooded man with a gun.

(MORE)

                              DYLAN (CONT'D)
          Women suspected of siding with the good guys. In most cases, just
          innocent women trying to protect their husbands and families.

Tears run down the side of Juliet's face.

                              DYLAN (CONT'D)
          If after a few Q & A sessions she didn't give the answers they
          wanted...

SIRENS can be heard from the street.

                              JULIET
          Stop it!

                              DYLAN
          My Kama Sutra sweetheart, you are interrupting my train of
          thought. If the girl was still physically able to speak after
          being beaten and raped, and lucky enough to say the right thing:
          magic! Her life was spared for the moment.

Dylan, his face now inches away from hers, as if they are about to kiss.

                         DYLAN (CONT'D)
          BAM!

Dylan releases the safety on the gun.

                              JULIET
          The police will be here any minute. Why don't you ask them about
          your Maya?

Dylan turns and aims his pistol at Juliet's head.

                              DYLAN
          Wrong fucking answer sweetheart!

                              JULIET
          The Paradise Hotel. There is an auction.

Dylan FIRES, blowing the head off the female figurine in the statue of the
erotic lovers, to the left of Juliet.

WINDOW

Dylan back steps to the window where he sees two police cars work their way
through heavy traffic.

Across from him Juliet lies back on the velvet couch.

                              DYLAN
          Just another day in paradise.

INT. JAMES'S BEDROOM - NIGHT

Tess tosses, turns, and then wakes abruptly. James turns over and kisses Tess on
the back of her neck.

                              JAMES
          Are you all right?

                              TESS
          I can't sleep.

Tess is at the edge of the bed. James pulls her into his arms.

                              JAMES
          Let me talk with my doctor. Maybe I can find something that helps
          put an end to these nightmares.

Tess gets up and steps toward the bathroom. Tears fill her eyes and she turns away from the mirror.

Tess angrily walks away from James and begins to put her things back into her bag.

                         JAMES (CONT'D)
     I'm heading south for a few days... ocean and beach. I would love
     to have you come along.

She turns and stares at his face.

                         TESS
     I... I need to get back to work. I haven't spoken to anyone in
     days.

James touches Tess from behind, running his hand between her legs.

                         TESS (CONT'D)
     Not now. I've got to get to the studio.

James clicks on the TV.

Tess walks into the bathroom to shower.

                    INDIAN ANCHORWOMAN
     The rash of hotel robberies continues. Over the past two weeks
     there have been seventeen robberies in major hotels in the Mumbai
     area. At this point, the police have no suspects.

The phone RINGS at the side of James's bed.

                         JAMES
     Good day, what gives me the pleasure?

James watches Tess step out of the shower.

                         JAMES (CONT'D)
     Is she going to press charges?

Tess walks out from the bathroom, drying her hair with a towel.

                         JAMES (CONT'D)
     Then it's out of my hands... Color-Tone Studio... Yes, I
     understand. I'll leave that up to you... Good day.

James hangs up the phone.

                         TESS
     What was that all about?

James watches Tess get dressed.

                              JAMES
          Looks like your camera jockey got a little out of hand last
          night. The police are looking for him, attempted murder.

                              TESS
          What?

                              JAMES
          They say he attacked the hostess at the Tantra Palace. Put a gun
          to her head. Took a shot at her but missed.

Tess, in shock, quickly pulls a T-shirt over her bare torso.

                              JAMES (CONT'D)
          The woman you asked me about?

                              TESS
          Your friend... Juliet?

Tess grabs her bag.

                              TESS (CONT'D)
          Your car?

James is about to throw her the keys, but doesn't.

                              JAMES
          I will drop you off on my way out.

EXT. SIDE STREET - PARADISE HOTEL - LATE NIGHT

Dylan exits his Jeep and heads for the entrance to the hotel.

INT. HOTEL - SAME

Dylan walks through the somewhat empty lobby and scopes the surroundings, puts
his shades back on and approaches the ELEVATOR OPERATOR.

                              DYLAN
          A party tonight... Girls?

The young elevator operator shakes his head in the typical yes /no gesture.

                              DYLAN (CONT'D)
          Excuse me, the floor number. I need the number to the fucking
          floor!

                              OPERATOR
          Ten.

Dylan casually pushes the elevator operator aside and marks nine. He removes his
cell phone from his pocket and dials.

INT. STAIRCASE CONTINUOUS

Dylan approaches the door to the tenth floor. Concealing himself, he looks through the glass.

INT. BALLROOM - CONTINUOUS

Dylan walks casually into a grand ballroom. The room is filled with thirty to forty GUESTS, mostly men and four or five women.

Drinks are served by a number of young mixed MALES. Overhead, boisterous bad electro-pop drowns the conversations into an unrecognizable buzz.

Dylan takes a drink from a tray and walks toward a group of men standing in front of a wall area surrounded by potted palms and cut flowers.

On the wall are dozens of eight-by-ten photos of young women and adolescent girls.

A number of MEN and TWO WOMEN stand in front of the photos. Some of the girls in the photos are naked from the waist up.

Black numbers marked at the bottom of each photo: twelve, fifteen, twenty-two and eighteen.

A stylish REDHEAD, perhaps Dutch, removes one of the photos. Dylan removes two photos, folds them and puts them in his jacket pocket.

A man in his early 50s, overweight and with a ruddy complexion, NORM PRESCOTT, approaches Dylan.

                         NORM
          Excuse me, I came here looking for... Oh, I'm Norm Prescott.

Dylan reluctantly shakes hands with him and then sips from his drink while viewing the stage.

                      NORM (CONT'D)
          I'm the manager of a garment factory in Sri Lanka. We lost half
          of our workers after that damn wave. I overheard someone talking
          downstairs about being able to find girls who could sew...

                        DYLAN
          I think you misunderstood. These girls are girls who are being--

The music stops a GONG is struck

Dylan downs the drink as Norm looks at Dylan strangely, then turns toward the stage.

Fifteen GIRLS in simple but new dresses are escorted to the stage. Printed tags with numbers around their necks.

A middle-aged ASIAN FEMALE HOSTESS catwalks to center stage.

                              HOSTESS
          Gentlemen, Ladies. Good evening. We have here a number of lovely
          ladies for you tonight. An exotic mix of Indian, Chinese, Thai,
          Cambodian and Nepalese.

Dylan hears a familiar voice.

Dylan watches Keith, standing with his back to the stage, with two men, an ARAB
and a young ASIAN in the middle of an unpleasant verbal exchange.

                         HOSTESS (CONT'D)
          You should all have already done your homework. All sales are
          final. The parcel is taken with the buyer when he leaves. All
          sales are made in cash. There are no refunds or exchanges,
          no damaged goods, or it doesn't quite fit. We assume that the
          majority of these young women are virgins.

She steps to the side and points to the rear of the stage.

                         HOSTESS (CONT'D)
          Number 126.

A GIRL, perhaps 12-years-old, the girl seen earlier on the bus with Maya, steps
to stage front. She is petrified.

                       MAN IN WICKER CHAIR
          Two thousand five hundred dollars.

There are no other bids.

                              HOSTESS
          Sold for two thousand five hundred dollars. Now number 128.

None of the girls move. The Hostess points toward a Chinese girl.

The Redhead, now smoking a cigarette, walks toward the stage, her eyes on the
prize.

                              REDHEAD
          One thousand six hundred and fifty!

A frightened smile takes over the girl's face.

                         REDHEAD (CONT'D)
          Can I see what I am buying?

                            MALE VOICE
          One thousand eight hundred and fifty!

The Hostess walks up to the young girl and takes the girl's dress and pulls it
up over her head, exposing the girl's naked torso. She motions for the girl to
turn around. The girl nervously sways and shimmies, in what seems like a move
that she copied from some lame hip-hop video.

                              REDHEAD
          They are all the same, a Chinese clone, same ass, same pear
          shaped tits. Centuries of inbreeding like fucking sheep, but she
          is a pretty one. How old?

The girl looks at the Hostess for a moment not knowing what to say. The Hostess
nods and holds up her fingers as if to count.

The young girl motions with five fingers, three times.

                              REDHEAD (CONT'D)
          Two thousand!

Chesterfield turns toward Dylan, smiling awkwardly with benign regret, and then
salutes him with a champagne toast.

INT. REAR OF BALLROOM - CONTINUOUS

Keith walks behind the potted plants and flowers. Bihari, in police uniform,
approaches. They talk for a moment. Bihari looks out toward Dylan as James
leaves the room.

                              HOSTESS
          Going once, going twice, sold for two thousand dollars!

The GONG sounds.

Dylan turns and again examines the remaining girls, hoping to find Maya.

TWO MEN suddenly grab Dylan from behind. A gun is shoved into his side and they
physically escort him toward James, who is standing alone in the corner at the
rear of the room.

James turns, opens a door and steps out into a rear hallway.

INT. HALLWAY - CONTINUOUS

The hoods shove Dylan out the door.

                              DYLAN
          Gentlemen, please get your hands off of me.

They escort him to where James is standing.

                              DYLAN (CONT'D)
          How is the nanny business?

                              JAMES (JOKINGLY)
          What a fine mess you have gotten yourself into, Mr. Jennings.

Dylan struggles to free himself from their grasp as Bihari laughs.

                              KIT
          He's looking for the girl from the restaurant.

                    JAMES
The girl you are looking for is not here. I am here for the same
reason that you are -- to make sure that nothing bad happens to
these girls.

                    DYLAN
Her father was murdered.

                    JAMES
Not her father and he was a wanted man. The girl you are looking
for is safe.

                    DYLAN
Au pair or a sex slave?

                    JAMES
Seems like our Mr. Jennings wants to play investigative reporter.

James lights a cigarette.

                    JAMES (CONT'D)
For the moment, we are two men involved in similar scenarios
-- Bengal tigers, beauty and ferocity. Young girls' beauty and
sexuality -- beauty and the beast. The tiger on the verge of
extinction. The young women in many third world cultures are an
endangered species -- not wanted or needed, just another mouth
to feed. The tiger ends up a man-made evolutionary dead-end.
The innocent young women become abandoned, sold, stolen. The
appropriate metaphor would be innocent lambs. Two versions of a
modern day example of supply and demand.

Dylan again goes after James but is barely held back.

                    JAMES (CONT'D)
The woman you should be worried about is...

Dylan tries to go after James again. This time James hits him hard in the
stomach. Dylan hunches over, struggling to catch his breath.

                    JAMES (CONT'D)
You have become an irritating fly on the wall. You had a smell, a
taste. It excites and teases you. You want to fuck them as much
as you want to save them. Get him and the rest of the girls the
hell out of here! If he knows about this, the police will be here
any minute.

The men drag Dylan down the hall. The elevator across from Dylan opens, a WOMAN
exits with a cart full of food. Dylan grabs the cart, knocks the two men off
their feet and dives inside the elevator.

INT. ELEVATOR - CONTINUOUS

The door closes. Dylan grimaces as he pushes the basement button. The door opens and the two hoods stand there with guns drawn.

EXT. REAR OF HOTEL - MOMENTS LATER

The two men push Dylan into the empty alley.

One of the men takes out his pistol and points it at the back of Dylan's head. Two quick SHOTS are fired. The two hoods fall to the ground, dead.

EXT. REAR OF HOTEL - FREIGHT ENTRANCE - CONTINUOUS

A figure in the shadow steps back into the hotel and the freight entrance door closes behind him.

EXT. REAR OF HOTEL - MOMENTS LATER

Dylan disappears down a dark side street.

EXT. STREET - CONTINUOUS

Dylan jumps into his Jeep, racing backwards down the street, knocking over food stands and carts.

People dive for cover. He does a three-point turn and speeds away.

INT. TANTRA PALACE - HOTEL ROOM - SAME

Maya sits in a large wicker chair. Behind her stands an Thai WOMAN, with her hands placed on Maya's shoulders.

In front of Maya is an elaborate bedroom ensemble. A middle-aged MAN and a young Thai WOMAN perform various sex acts.

A large pair of blue doors swings open and Juliet walks in.

                         JULIET
          Well, well, my sweet Maya.

Maya gets up from the chair, her eyes dilated.

Juliet removes the sleeping gown that Maya is wearing.

                       INDIAN WOMAN
          Her English is impeccable.

She walks around Maya, who stands frozen. Juliet slowly places a red rose in her hair.

                         JULIET
          My little Princess. I had hoped that you would be one of our
          favorite girls. The car is waiting for her downstairs.

EXT. ENTRANCE TO COLOR-TONE STUDIO - EARLY EVENING

Dylan exits the studio. Two INDIAN POLICEMEN approach.

                         POLICEMAN #1
     Mr. Jennings.

Dylan stops.

                         POLICEMAN #2
     We would like to take you for a little ride.

                              DYLAN
     I was about to get a bite to eat.

Dylan smiles, turns and breaks into a sprint through cross town traffic.

EXT. STREET - CONTINUOUS

The chase is fast and furious through a crowded maze of stalls, shopkeepers, holy cows and traffic of every imaginable configuration.

Dylan is running so fast he can hardly breathe. The younger Policeman catches up to him, knocking him to the ground.

Dylan manages to pull himself up to a standing position.

                    YOUNGER POLICE OFFICER
     Don't move!

                              DYLAN
     I'm still hungry.

The younger Policeman cuffs Dylan.

                    OLDER POLICE OFFICER
     Mr. Jennings. Have you ever heard of Nan and water?

INT. COLOR-TONE STUDIO - LATER

Tess enters the studio. The secretary is agitated. Remi stands waiting to be heard.

                              REMI
     He came back about an hour ago. He was fucking nuts.

                              TESS
     About what?

                              REMI
     Yesterday evening he said he knew where they took the girl,
     started talking about an auction. He also started talking about
     the guy you have been seeing. Your Mr. Guardian.

She pulls out her cell phone and dials a number.

                              REMI (CONT'D)
          Fifteen minutes ago two of Mumbai's finest showed up looking for
          him.

                              TESS
          James, it's me. Any news?

INT. GUARDIAN'S OFFICE - SAME

James stands in front of a large window that looks out at the harbor area of
Mumbai. He focuses on a container that is being unloaded from the back of a
truck.

                              JAMES
          I talked with the police about the girl. So far, no word.

INT. NEWS OFFICE - SAME

Tess picks up Dylan's bag and empties it out onto a table as she continues to
talk on the phone.

                              JAMES (V.O.)
          The police are looking for your cameraman.

She picks up the photos that Dylan took from the hotel auction and she finds a
copy of the photo of James and the girls.

INT. GUARDIAN'S OFFICE - SAME

James turns as Juliet hands him a package of airline tickets.

                              JAMES
          The list of missing persons in this city is like a fucking
          telephone book.

                              TESS
          I will call you later.

INT. NEWS OFFICE - SAME

Tess hangs up the phone and walks past Remi, who is playing a computer game on a
monitor.

Tess walks toward another monitor at the other end of the room and clicks into
her email. She scrolls forward, the photo of the dead girl fills the screen.

                              TESS
          My God.

Phone RINGS.

The secretary enters the room holding a fax that she gives to Remi.

                              SECRETARY
          A message from Police Headquarters.

                                REMI
          Shit. They have him. Booked him on attempted murder and resisting
          arrest. I think you may have the story that you have been looking for.

                              SECRETARY
          A taxi is waiting downstairs.

Tess clicks off the computer. Tess and Remi head toward the elevator.

EXT. STREET IN FRONT OF CNN - CONTINUOUS

Tess and Remi jump into a waiting taxi.

                                TESS
          Police Headquarters, please.

Tess stares out the window. A CHILD sips water from a leaking hydrant.

                           TESS (CONT'D)
          I should have gone with him.

Tess takes her hotel room card and laptop from her bag.

                                REMI
          I can only imagine what he's putting those poor bastards through
          at Police Headquarters.

                                TESS
          I want you to take this and go back to his hotel room. Stay there
          until I call you.

                                REMI
          No, I want to...

Tess gives him the don't-say-another-word look. Remi places the room card and
laptop in his bag.

EXT. STREET CORNER - BENGAL HOTEL - CONTINUOUS

Taxi comes to a jerking halt.

Tess hands the DRIVER some Thai notes. Just as Remi is about to get out, Tess
puts Dylan's bag in Remi's lap and closes the door.

                                TESS
          I will meet you back at the hotel. (To the cab driver) The Oberoi.

          Thank you.

The taxi slowly pulls away. EXT. DOCK AREA - SAME

The container seen earlier is being loaded onto a cargo ship.

A close up of the container shows peep holes cut into the side of the container.

CLOSE-UP

Eyes peek through two of the holes. INT. CONTAINER - CONTINUOUS

Light filters through a number of holes.

Two young girls illuminated by the light sit eating a small piece of melon.

The container is filled with twenty to thirty wooden beds stacked on top of each other.

Some of the girls were previously seen at the auction. A number of the girls are as young as 10 or 11-years-old. A narrow walkway runs between the two rows of beds. A porta-san (portable toilet) sits at the end of the walkway.

A medium-sized box filled with pieces of bread, a number of plastic six-packs of water and an assortment of overripe fruit rest on the floor.

EXT. STREET OUTSIDE RESTAURANT - LATER

Tess walks through a steady rain.

INT. MOHAN'S RESTAURANT - CONTINUOUS

Tess pushes the front door of the restaurant open. Tess goes through the kitchen, removing a container of water from a glass case as she heads toward the living area of the unit.

Tess walks into Maya's tiny room. The interior is empty.

EXT. STREET - MOMENTS LATER

CHILDREN scavenge through trash at the rear of the restaurant.

The rain has stopped. Tess pauses and lights a cigarette. A MOTORCYCLE with Keith wearing head phones, speeds up and circles her twice, then blocks her path.

Tess steps around Keith and heads toward Tapti Street.

                              KEITH
          You're the Tiger Lady, yes?

He moves the bike to block her path.

                         KEITH (CONT'D)
          I think that it may be a good time to end this wonderful, exotic,
          sometimes sexy adventure of yours. You do not want to end up like
          those poor tigers you can't find.

                                   TESS
          I'm not ready to leave yet. It may be a good time for you to stop
          smoking.

A BUS pulls up at the street corner in front of her.

Tess takes the cigarette from her mouth, has one last puff, and effortlessly
puts it out on Keith's cheek.

Keith jerks, SCREAMS, and he and the bike topple to the pavement.

BUS

Tess boards the bus with a number of INDIAN WOMEN. The bus pulls away.

INT. POLICE HOLDING AREA - SAME

The office has the appearance of a vast storehouse. It is damp and dirty.
Resigned PEOPLE crowd benches lining the perimeter walls.

INT. WORK STATION - CONTINUOUS

A young OFFICER with a nightstick sits a few feet away. Dylan sits agitated,
repeatedly trying to free his cuffed hands from the back of the metal chair.

                                  DYLAN
          I didn't do a fucking thing. Look in my bag. I don't have a
          weapon!

MILA, a young female officer, approaches from behind.

                                  MILA
          You didn't have a bag.

                                  DYLAN
          Listen to me. A young girl was kidnapped. Her father, or whoever
          the hell he was, has been murdered. I can identify the men. One
          of them was... I think he was a cop.

The young officer pushes Dylan back into his seat.

                              DYLAN (CONT'D)
          I know this is not news to you, but there are some very powerful
          scumbags out there who are selling young girls like they're
          fucking cattle.

                                  MILA
          Not like cattle. We cherish our cattle... They are sold like used
          cars.

INT. POLICE HOLDING AREA - SAME

Dylan continues to rant.

                              DYLAN
          Is everyone deaf around here? I witnessed a murder and
          kidnapping!

Mila approaches Dylan and the two officers.

                              MILA
          Our only concern is that you tried to kill a woman with a gun.

INT. POLICE RECEPTION AREA - CONTINUOUS

Tess enters the Mumbai Police Headquarters and heads toward, but does not
actually stop at, the reception desk.

                              TESS
          A friend of mine, an American, was arrested. Where can I find
          him?

                              DESK SERGEANT
          Try C.I.D., third floor.

The MAN at the front desk pages through a ledger and calls after her.

                              DESK SERGEANT (CONT'D)
          Madame, you see Superintendent Shiva Mahadev. But you know, you
          can only talk to your friend. He will be staying with us for some
          time. I will inform Mr. Mahadev that you are on your way.

INT. HOLDING AREA - SAME

                              MILA
          You did have a weapon. You blew one of the lovers heads off. This
          is not New York City, Mr. Jennings.

                              DYLAN
          I'm going to be charged for killing a fucking statue?!

                              MILA
          So, you did have a gun? Thank you, Mr. Jennings.

Dylan stands up, DRAGGING the chair with him towards Mila.

                              DYLAN
          Maybe when no one was looking I stuck it up my ass!

Dylan leans across the table, staring Mila in the face.

                              DYLAN (CONT'D)
          Are you telling me that the kidnapping and selling of a 14-year-
          old child doesn't even raise a fucking eyebrow?

                              MILA
          Listen to me. Once I have your confession, I will pass along what
          you have written to the proper channels. That is all I can do.

INT. UPPER FLOOR - POLICE HEADQUARTERS - SAME

Tess continues to wander dank corridors. A particularly dark corridor has a long
bench occupied by numerous WOMEN.

One of the women on the floor is Shanti's mother, Lakshmi.

                         LAKSHMI
     Memsahib, memsahib!

Lakshmi walks into the room. Mila, seated behind an ancient desk covered in
stacks of paper.

                         MILA
     Would you mind queuing like everyone else?

                         TESS
     I just need to know where the C.I.D. is. A friend has been
     arrested. Do you have a holding tank?

                         MILA
     This is not a fish market.

                         TESS
     Thank you for your help.

Tess finally notices Lakshmi.

                         LAKSHMI
     They kill my husband!

                         TESS
     Sorry about what happened.

Tess scans the line of other women. Many of the women are clutching forms and
photos of young girls.

                         LAKSHMI
     We agreed to take her for the four thousand rupia that they gave
     for taking children after the wave. I am her aunt. We needed the
     money. Mr. Guardian had a family that would hire her.

Tess looks at Lakshmi.

                         TESS
     Mr. Guardian was going to send her abroad?

Lakshmi nods agreeing as Tess removes the photo from her pocket.

                         LAKSHMI
     The men who killed my Mohan and who stole Maya, they worked for
     your Mr. Guardian.

Tess notices the office door is marked in English and Hindu: "Female Protection Unit."

Tess takes Lakshmi by the arm and walks her into Mila's office.

                              MILA
          Listen, I thought I told you there is a line.

                              TESS
          Look, this woman's child was taken away by the police. Her
          husband killed. I knew the girl.

Mila looks at Lakshmi, then at Tess.

                              MILA
          You have a friend, a Mr. Jennings?

Lakshmi hands Tess a bloodstained business card reading, "Overseas Placement."
The two women exchange a questioning stare.

                              MILA (CONT'D)
          Many families sign contracts to have their children work abroad.
          We know your Mr. Guardian. From what I understand, not as well as
          you do.

                              TESS
          What exactly do you mean by that?

                              MILA
          Your Mr. Guardian is what you would refer to as a major player.

Tess walks over to the large clipboard on the wall, looking at pictures and
newspaper clippings of other violent acts against women and children.

                              MILA (CONT'D)
          We know very well who he is and what he does. If he broke the
          law, he would be arrested. Just like your Mr. Jennings. As for the
          girl, you will have to file a missing persons report.

Mila looks at Tess and then at Lakshmi.

                              MILA (CONT'D)
          When you work here you don't have to go to the movies. Much
          of this society still lives by practices that should have been
          outlawed hundreds of years ago. There are over two hundred
          thousand female prostitutes in Mumbai, many of them under the age
          of 14.

                              TESS
          What about these two?

She picks up the photo of two young girls, the two girls seen at the village a
few days ago.

                                MILA
        The elders of this village decided to sell these two so they
        could buy a satellite dish. We went to the village to investigate,
        the girls' relatives claimed that they ran away. If they're lucky,
        they are now cleaning toilets in Bahrain. And the village gets to
        watch the weekly exploits of *Bay Watch*.

Mila opens another drawer and pulls out a pile of forms and hands them to
Lakshmi.

                                MILA (CONT'D)
        There is not much more I can tell you. You must follow
        procedures, and I would suggest you find a good lawyer.

Lakshmi glibly accepts the forms, walks to a table in the corner, and starts
filling them out.

                                MILA (CONT'D)
        Criminal Investigation. The next corridor, make a right.

Tess exchanges a glance with Mila and walks out the door and into the next
office.

INT. OFFICE - MOMENTS LATER

                                TESS
        I want to see Mr. Jennings.

                                OFFICER
        You will not be able to see him until Monday. The jail is closed,
        this is a holy weekend.

Bihari follows Tess into the other office.

                                BIHARI
        The young girl was taken away because Mohan's wife was the girl's
        aunt. They took money they could not pay back. Mohan was killed
        in self-defense after he attacked me with a knife.

Bihari watches as Mila talks with Lakshmi.

                                BIHARI (CONT'D)
        And please tell him that people with too much information, of the
        wrong kind, tend to vanish. How do you say?

Bihari snaps his fingers.

                                BIHARI (CONT'D)
        In a Mumbai minute.

EXT. STREET - OPEN TAXI - THREE DAYS LATER

Tess sits in the rear of a three-wheel taxi as it zigzags through crowded
streets.

EXT. OFFICE BUILDING - AN HOUR LATER.

Tess walks past the front of a building; it looks empty. She goes to the front
entrance and reads the index, Overseas Placements, fourth floor. A GUARD inside
is watching TV.

INT. BUILDING - HALLWAY

Tess climbs stairs. She pauses at a window on the fourth floor. Juliet, in
casual dress, is getting ready to leave the office.

Photos of girls and James accent the desk and walls. Juliet smiles as she gets
up from the desk and lets her in.

INT. OFFICE - SAME

                              JULIET
          Is there something that I can help you with?

                               TESS
          I was looking for James.

Tess slowly patrols the office looking at the photos on the walls.

                          TESS (CONT'D)
          All of these women, these young girls...

                              JULIET
          Yes, they all have been part of Mr. Guardian's business.

                               TESS
          Mr. Guardian is a very busy man.

Tess walks toward Juliet at her desk and removes the photo of James and the
young girls seen earlier.

                          TESS (CONT'D)
          You're not much older than many of these young woman.

Juliet looks at the photo and the younger image of herself standing next to
Guardian.

                              JULIET
          I was one of these young women.

                               TESS
          What's you relationship with James... now?

                              JULIET
          No I do not sleep with him... not anymore. He saved my life. At
          the age of 14, I was sold by my father to the owner of a KTV bar
          in Shanghai. Six months later after servicing a man and two of his
          business associates, I was promised a job at a sneaker factory.
          The following night, James was one of my customers. He told me I
          was about to be sold as a sex slave to the owner of that sneaker
          company and his friends.

Juliet turns the computer back on and pulls up a file.

                              JULIET (CONT'D)
          This business, the skin trade, has been going on forever.
          Sometimes it can be a blessing. An actual job, a roof over your
          head, steady food in your stomach. But most of the time it is
          your worst nightmare.

Tess gives her a disgusted look as Juliet opens a file.

                              JULIET (CONT'D)
          James told me about what happened in Africa.

Juliet steps away from the desk and walks toward the window.

                              JULIET (CONT'D)
          It is very hot in here.

Juliet opens the window.

                              TESS
          Why did you press charges against my cameraman?

                              JULIET
          Because he tried to kill me. You both come here, meet some
          teenager who you know nothing about, and suddenly she becomes,
          how do you say it, your cause celebre.

Juliet goes back to her desk and pulls back her chair all most offering Tess a
seat.

                              JULIET (CONT'D)
          Are you actually interested in trying to change things or is it
          the rush of another big story?

                              TESS
          And what if I said both?

                              JULIET
          Could you pardon me a minute? I have to use the loo.

DOOR

Juliet nods to Tess and closes the door as she leaves. Tess stands looking down
at the computer monitor.

The phone RINGS.

EXT. DECK AT COUNTRY CLUB - SAME

James, with cell phone, looks confidently out over a lush garden and the haze of
the city beyond.

INT. JAMES'S OFFICE

Tess stands frozen as the phone RINGS.

A car door SLAMS and there is some TALKING. Tess walks to the window and peers
out.

Her expression changes dramatically. The answering machine begins to record the
call.

> JAMES (V.O.)
> Juliet, I want you to call the Mumbai Police Headquarters,
> Officer Shanji. They are holding an American, a Mr. Jennings. Tell
> him that I want to make sure that he is taken care of properly.
> If Ms. Douglas calls, tell her that I will be away for a few days.

Tess goes back to the window. Keith speaks with two Arab-looking men.

INT. OFFICE DESK - MONITOR - CONTINUOUS

Tess views photos similar to the photos on display at the auction: Asian,
Caucasian, Slavic, African, some of the groups are indicated by countries,
Cambodia, India, Nepal, and Vietnam. Spreadsheets manifest between some of the
files: a column of numbers followed by one of letter codes, a third column of
currency amounts in the thousands.

EXT. HALLWAY - CONTINUOUS

With her other hand, Tess fumbles wildly through her bag finally removing a
memory stick.

Tess turns and looks at the open window as the computer copies the files to the
stick

She races though more files: more women's faces, including Maya's, flash across
the screen.

INT. HALLWAY - SAME

NOISE from the hallway. Keith is SINGING some rap song.

                                    TESS
          Come on, come on.

EXT. WINDOW - SAME

The office door opens as Tess falls flat onto the fire escape landing.

Juliet and Keith enter the office. Juliet smiles, looks around the office, and
nervously goes back to her desk.

Keith opens a desk drawer and removes a pack of air tickets. Loud NOISE from the
street.

Juliet notices that the window is open.

                                    KEITH
          That son of a bitch left no money.

                                    JULIET
          All I was given were the tickets and visas.

Juliet walks over to the window and looks out onto the fire escape and sees
Tess. Juliet closes the window.

FIRE ESCAPE - MOMENTS LATER

Tess carefully works her way down the fire escape.

OFFICE

Keith heads toward the door.

                                    KEITH
          If you hear from him...tell him we have a problem.

INT. OFFICE - MOMENTS LATER

Juliet stands at the front office window. Looking down, she sees Tess walking
across the street.

STREET

Tess stops a taxi, turns and looks up at the office window. Juliet and Tess
exchange a thankful smile.

Tess enters the taxi and leaves.

INT. POLICE STATION - HOLDING AREA - TUESDAY

Several inactive office ATTENDANTS are seated at desks, one of them is
especially old, with a white beard and turban.

At several desks, there are SUSPECTS in handcuffs and foot irons, LAWYERS,
pleading RELATIVES and irritated and tired police OFFICERS.

                              TESS

     You have an American.

                         OLD ATTENDANT

     Oh, yes, follow me please.

INT. HOLDING AREA - DYLAN'S TABLE - SAME

Tess sits down as Dylan is brought out into the holding area and is again
handcuffed to the chair.

                              DYLAN

     Did you get lost or just decide I needed a little jail time R and
     R?

Tess scans the room, stopping suddenly as Bihari, in police uniform, enters the
office.

                              TESS

     It was a holiday. I couldn't get in. Why were you harassing one of
     James's friends with a gun?

Tess pauses for a moment as Mila walks through the corridor. Mila stops and
talks with the young officer who arrested Dylan. The officer gives her Dylan's
paperwork.

                              DYLAN

     I saw them take her.

                              TESS

     The girl was taken because the money should not have been paid.
     They were fucking family.

                              DYLAN

     This au pair nonsense is bull shit. I went to an auction. A
     fucking auction where they sell young girls.

Tess watches as Bihari enters the room behind her.

                         TESS (softly)

     Shut the fuck up and listen to me. Do not talk!

Mila and another police officer approach as Bihari watches from a distance.

                         TESS (CONT'D)

     I just left his office. Thousands of girls and young women on
     file. Letters, family photographs. (Louder wanting to be heard) I
     think you are wrong about Guardian. He looks clean.

                              DYLAN

     Right, about as clean as a Mumbai street. Your new boy toy was at
     the fucking auction

Tess and Mila look at each other. Mila nods toward the older officer.

Tess walks over to a short, overweight man, SUPERINTENDENT SHIVA MAHADEV.

                           TESS
          Excuse me, sir. I am an American. There has been a mistake.

                           MAHADEV
          No mistake. Your friend, Mr. Jennings, has been charged with
          attempted murder.

Mila stands at Tess's side.

                           MILA
          She is aware of that.

Mila motions toward the policeman as a SCREAMING argument starts between two
parties on either side of the room.

The policeman walks toward Dylan and Tess with key in hand, removes the cuffs
and stands at attention behind Dylan.

INT. OTHER SIDE OF ROOM - CONTINUOUS

                           TESS
          How much money will this take?

                           MAHADEV
          I think you should put the money away, your friend is going to be
          with us...

                           MILA
          Remove his handcuffs. I have papers from our court-appointed
          lawyer for him to sign.

An INDIAN WOMAN with a shawl covering her face rises from her seat, takes the
ink well from her desk and hurls it at a YOUNG ATTORNEY. It misses his head.
GLASS EXPLODES against the wall. The argument becomes louder.

A MAN rushes over and knocks an attorney to the ground with one punch.
Pandemonium breaks out. The officer, Mila and Mahadev run toward the action.

Dylan pulls Tess to the floor. Chairs fly over their heads. Someone is slammed
across the table and onto the floor.

Dylan and Tess crawl toward the door.

Exiting, they disappear into heavy pedestrian traffic.

INT - POLICE HOLDING AREA - SAME

As the police and Mila attempt to brake up the fight, the Thai woman removes the
head scarf and heads for the door. It is Juliet.

INT. DYLAN'S JEEP - MINUTES LATER.

Dylan and Tess drive through Mumbai. Dylan is driving much too fast for the slow moving, congested traffic.

                              DYLAN
          You sleep with this scumbag and keep insisting that he is clean.
          Am I missing something here?

Tess emotionally sorts through this nefarious nightmare that has encircled them.

                              DYLAN (CONT'D)
          I have heard of denial, but this is...

Tess looks disparagingly at Dylan, not wanting to hear what he is about to say.

                              DYLAN (CONT'D)
          Were you listening to me earlier? This was no fashion show, no
          pageant. They were selling women, young girls. Guardian was there.

                              TESS
          Files with family photos, thank you letters.

EXT. DEAD END STREET - HOTEL - CONTINUOUS

Dylan pulls the car to a stop.

                              TESS
          I went with him up into the hills north of the city to an
          orphanage. The Sisters and children treated him like he was a
          saint.

The car sits idle as ahead of them a number of ghost-like figures in white cross the dark street.

                              TESS (CONT'D)
          We already know that relief organizations here are not run like
          the Red Cross.

                              DYLAN
          Relief organizations? You've got to be fucking kidding me.

Tess looks at him gently, touching the side of his face with the backside of her hand.

                              TESS
          The asshole who threatened me. He was in Guardian's office. There
          is obviously a connection and the other is a...

                              DYLAN
          A dirty cop.

EXT. ALLURE GUEST HOUSE - LATE AFTERNOON

Tess and Dylan stand at the entrance to a narrow alleyway, half hidden by a construction site.

Dylan pulls her into his arms and they embrace. Tess steps back and adjusts her self.

                    TESS
     Did you see her at the auction?

Dylan shakes his head no.

                    DYLAN
     Before I was taken away to be wasted, Guardian said something
     about her being safe. No. I didn't see her. But what the fuck does
     that mean?!

Dylan steps back and wipes the tears from her eyes. Tess kisses him.

                    TESS
     I think it's time we pass on what you know to the authorities and
     get the hell out of here.

Dylan removes the gun from his pants and holds it in front of Tess.

                    DYLAN
     Let me show you how to use this.

Tess takes the gun from his hand, turning it, holding it as if it was part of her anatomy.

                    TESS
     I shot at targets with my ex-husband's picture on it for months
     after he betrayed me.

Tess holds the gun, firmly pointing it at Dylan's chest.

                    TESS (CONT'D)
     This is the safety, release it to fire. The clip has twelve shots.
     Hold it with both hands, tightly!

Tess clicks on the safety and sticks it in the front of her pants.

                    Tess (CONT'D)
     We can't go back to the police.

Tess pretends to collect herself.

                    TESS (CONT'D)
     What are you going to do?

                    DYLAN
     We have the information you need. This story will be huge.

Tess shows Dylan the memory stick she holds in her hand.

                              TESS
          Maybe you're right.

                              DYLAN
          I will call you when I have everything arranged.

Dylan kisses her softly on the lips.

INT. ALLURE HOTEL - FRONT DESK

Tess counts out money from her purse.

A PORTER, in greasy rags, starts lugging her bags up a CREAKING staircase. Tess
follows him as the DESK CLERK calls after her.

                              DESK CLERK
          Would you like something to eat or drink?

Tess climbs the stairs, her back soaked with perspiration as the porter
mumbles something to himself.

                              TESS
          A bottle of water.

HOTEL ROOM

The electricity flickers and then goes out. Tess lights two candles. The door to
the balcony is open.

RAIN has begun to fall as Tess lies down on the bed. Thunder quietly RUMBLES.
Tess closes her eyes.

SUPER: INT. BUS STATION - DARFUR - SIXTEEN MONTHS AGO

A truck load of young soldiers skids to a stop. The ragtag unit of teenage males
climbs out of the truck.

SIDE STREET

Tess and Dylan continue down a narrow side street. In front of them, GODIE
motions for them to follow.

A door flings wide open as SOLDIERS come out of adjoining rooms and run past
them.

                              GODIE
          Stop!

Dylan reaches his hand out to Tess. GUNFIRE explodes in all directions.

                              DYLAN
          Where the fuck are we going?

                              TESS
          The boy says he knows where they have the hostages.

                              DYLAN
          Then why don't we go and tell the--

HALLWAY

                              TESS
          There are no good guys here. The government troops are as bad as
          the insurgents...can you tell the difference between one dickhead
          and the other?

Godie pokes Tess with his rifle and shakes his head no.

                              TESS
          These women have been held captive for over six months. The kid
          says he knows where they are. We find them, it's our story.

Godie stops by Tess walking through the open hole in the wall.

ABANDONED ROOM

                              DYLAN
          You really think that they're going to allow us to just walk in
          and out of here?

                              TESS
          Only one way to find out.

Tess eyes Godie, who enters another hallway, SHOOTING bullets into a young
government soldier.

Other soldiers exit the room.

Tess is knocked to the floor. Struggling she turns over, somewhat dazed. Godie
and the Dutch women stand in front of her.

                              GODIE
          You will be safe now.

EXT. MAINTENANCE BUILDING

Insurgents break from one of the smaller buildings. Government soldiers in
secured positions turn it into a turkey shoot.

MAIN BUILDING

Tess hears someone CRYING. A Government soldier sits in the corner hiding. One
of the Dutch girls lies dead at his feet.

                              TESS
          No!

Soldiers continue to exchange GUNFIRE with a few remaining insurgents. Dylan walks out of the station house, camera in hand, looking for Tess.

U.N. Helicopter circles the area above the treetops, spraying the ground area with GUNFIRE.

HELICOPTER

The pilot pokes the gunner and they look down at the main building and Dylan.

YARD

Dylan waves his arms over his head as the helicopter approaches.

                              DYLAN (SCREAMING)
          We have found the hostages!

The helicopter swoops low past Dylan. He flattens himself out on the ground.

INT. STATION HOUSE - CONTINUOUS

Godie walks slowly toward Tess with blood oozing from his shoulder and chest; his weapon hangs loosely at his side. Godie staggers as the helicopter hovers above them.

Tess grabs hold of Godie, and they break for the open door.

EXT. YARD - SAME

The four Dutch captives follow behind them. Tess stops and reaches back for one of the young women.

SHOTS are fired around them.

Dylan films as Godie staggers a few feet ahead of Tess.

Tess turns around. The other women have headed back to the shelter of the building.

Godie grabs at Tess pulling her forward away from the building.

SKY

The helicopter turns and fires two rockets. BAM-BAM! The building EXPLODES, the blasts knock Tess and Godie to the ground.

STATION HOUSE - YARD

SHOTS come from behind the building. The copter gets hit, gyrates wildly in the sky and then CRASHES into a row of mud and tin houses.

Godie lies next to Tess. Tess struggles to rise as Dylan approaches.

Tess turns Godie's frail body over, feeling for a pulse, wiping dirt and blood from his face.

                              TESS
        Did they get out?

Tess rises awkwardly as Godie lies lifeless at her feet.

                         TESS (CONT'D)
        What happened? Where the fuck did they go?

A U.N. assault vehicle and Jeep pull up behind Dylan and Tess. Troops sweep the area.

One of the Government soldiers talks with another soldier, pointing toward the station house, then at Dylan and Tess.

The officer walks from the smoldering remains, looking coldly at Tess and Dylan, kicking at what's left of Dylan's video camera.

                            OFFICER
        We had plans to clear this area. This morning, we had made a deal
        with them.

Tess observes the patchwork of dead bodies, including the bodies of two of the Dutch women.

                        OFFICER (CONT'D)
        You're supposed to report the fucking news, not create it.

Dylan stands motionless. Tess steps back as a U.N. photographer takes a photo of Tess, Dylan and the officer standing over the body of Godie.

A gust of wind moves the smoke like a halo over the scattered remains.

SUPER. HOTEL ROOM - PRESENT

The wind BLOWS her door shut. Tess jerks awake.

The glass beads and fringe, hanging from the entwined lover's desk lamp, gently RATTLE.

                              MIRROR
Clutching the gun in both hands pointing at her reflection in the mirror.

BROKEN GLASS - LATER

Stepping from the shower, Tess puts on pants and a T-shirt, picks up the phone, dials.

                              TESS
        It's me. We need to talk.

EXT. TANTRA PALACE - LATER

An old SOLDIER stands guard with a rifle. Tess slips him a five rupee note and walks on in.

Tess climbs a circular staircase toward a U-shaped balcony overlooking a well-manicured garden.

EXT. GARDEN - TANTRA PALACE - SAME

A number of YOUNG WOMEN and GIRLS pose against erotic sculptures in the lush garden.

Tess's eyes click off their images like the shutter of a camera. Maya is not among them.

The girls turn and disappear into the night.

INT. HALLWAY - MOMENTS LATER

Tess opens doors of empty rooms, decorated in Victorian opulence with Thai accents.

Tess continues her search. The next room has a Caucasian MALE with bad sunburn, seated on the edge of a bed. A young GIRL lies between his legs.

Chesterfield looks up at Tess as she enters the room.

                         TESS
          You son of a bitch!

                         CHESTERFIELD
          Come on. You know the third world better than any of us! For the
          majority of these girls, it beats starving to death.

Chesterfield tries to compose himself.

                         CHESTERFIELD (CONT'D)
          You and Jennings are fucking with the wrong people.

They both stare at each other for a moment.

                         TESS
          We got so close. He told me we should stop, but I kept trying to
          push the door open and now he is--

                         CHESTERFIELD
          If I were you, I would get the fuck out of here. Their goondas
          make our wise guys look like school boys.

Tess pulls the gun from the back of her pants.

                         TESS
          Having this child pinned between your legs makes you feel more
          like a man?

Tess lowers the gun. Chesterfield begins laughing.

                              CHESTERFIELD
          You still want to play martyr, save the world and all that bull
          shit.

                              TESS
          Fuck you!

Tess motions for the young girl to leave, she stays and moves toward
Chesterfield.

                              CHESTERFIELD
          Forgive me... but I am an emotionally dead man.

Tess exits and crosses over to the other side of the hallway.

A door is opened by a middle-aged white MAN. Two girls sit on the bed beside
him. He quickly closes the door.

INT. OFFICE - MOMENTS LATER

Tess roams through Juliet's office. Car doors SLAM.

Tess looks out the open window. Bihari and another INDIAN MALE head toward the
doorway.

The VOICES of the two men can now be heard. The two men enter the office.

EXT. WINDOW - SAME

Tess drops from the open window onto the fire escape.

INT. JEEP - MOMENTS LATER

Tess's Jeep SLAMS into parked cars on either side of her. STREET

Bihari and the other man run down the street in her direction with guns drawn.
SHOTS are fired.

Tess shifts into drive and SCREECHES out into traffic.

EXT. MUMBAI - RAIN - MOMENTS LATER

Tess's Jeep moves through the heart of the city.

Thousands of umbrellas form an almost continuous roof over the streets. MEN in
clean white dhotis daintily lift the slips of their garments as they traverse
puddles.

WORKING WOMEN, with heavy loads on their heads, move about in their drenched
saris.

CHILDREN play in the gutters which have turned into flowing streams.

INT. JAMES'S APARTMENT - EVENING

Tess stands looking out the window at two young lovers making out in an
alleyway. James sits behind her on a couch.

                              JAMES
          Why were you were in my office?

Tess turns and walks slowly toward James. James stares at her. A brief silence.

                              TESS
          You certainly make it look like just another business.

                              JAMES
          How are you feeling? I talked to a doctor friend about your
          nightmares.

James reaches out and gently touches her face. Tess pulls away.

                              TESS
          Dylan claims that there was a an auction, an auction that you
          attended.

James looks at his reflection in the mirror.

                              JAMES
          It is one of the ways we try to find out who the players... and
          your friend was not an invited guest.

                              TESS
          The girl from the restaurant?

                              JAMES
          Your cameraman's girlfriend?

                              TESS
          She's 14-years-old.

                              JAMES
          That's who he wanted when he nearly shot Juliet.

Tess walks toward him and shakes her head in disgust.

                              TESS
          Maya, you brought her to Mumbai?

                              JAMES
          Them to Mumbai, I brought a number of bus loads of girls after
          the tsunami.

Tess walks to the other side of the desk.

James pours two drinks. He offers Tess a drink; she takes it and walks away.

                              JAMES (CONT'D)
I have tried to show you that you have no story and that I run a
very legitimate business.

                                TESS
I saw the *Newsweek* article, the girls who were found murdered in
Miami. There was a photo of you with the two girls. You got them
into the States.

                               JAMES
Sometimes a percentage of the traffic has to fall through the
cracks. At times we have to look as bad as the scumbags we are
trying to close down.

                                TESS
That sounds exactly like what I would tell a reporter, especially
one I was fucking.

Tess downs the drink.

                             TESS (CONT'D)
What I need to find out is if Maya is a part of the small percent
that make your business look legit, or if she is on her way to
some brothel or sex slave?

James walks toward Tess. He takes the empty drink from her hand and gently
separates her hair from her shoulder and in his best George Clooney.

                               JAMES
You want an up ending to your story. Take the expressway maybe
fifteen miles north of the city, not far from the preserve. The
Star Dust Hotel, you can't miss it. There are a group of girls.
They will be leaving tomorrow for the States. Your Maya is there.
Ask them anything you like, and maybe, before he leaves, your
cameraman can finally taste the young--

James catches Tess's hand before she slaps his face and leans forward kissing
her on the lips.

EXT. OBEROI HOTEL - MINUTES LATER

Tess pulls up in front of the Oberoi Hotel. She exits the vehicle and heads
toward the entrance.

INT. NINTH FLOOR - CONTINUOUS

Tess gets off the elevator and heads toward Dylan's room. There is commotion in
the hallway.

Two MEN come out the room door, carrying a body bag on a stretcher.

                                TESS
What happened?

Tess walks toward the stretcher, but is stopped.

                              MALE COP
         Male victim. One gunshot to the head. A friend of yours?

The elevator door closes leaving Tess alone in the corridor with a few hotel
staff.

INT. JEEP - MOMENTS LATER

Tess sits crying as the Jeep idles for a moment in front of the hotel. Dylan's
Yankee cap lies in the empty seat next to her.

EXT. TRAFFIC - MINUTES LATER

The traffic light changes as Tess pulls out and blends in with the congested
maze of traffic.

INT. BEDROOM - STAR DUST HOTEL - SAME

Sitting under the window in a room, Maya nervously tries to comb out her hair
with her hand. There are ten to twelve other GIRLS with her: a mix of Chinese,
Nepalese and Thai.

Five of them are lying on one bed, two sit talking in the bathroom. There are
clothes, debris and food scraps on the floor, along with ten to fifteen empty
bottles of water.

Two of the Chinese-looking girls sit across from her on the floor. One of them
is crying.

Neither one can speak the other's language.

                         GIRL ON BED (THAI)
         We both come from Phuket.

Maya watches an INDIAN GIRL leave the bathroom.

                              INDIAN GIRL
         Anyone have any napkins, toilet paper?

A few of the girls shake their heads no. The Thai girls look at each other, not
knowing what was said.

The Thai girl looks out the window where a MAN pulls into the yard on a Vespa,
carrying a black doctor's bag.

                         INDIAN GIRL (CONT'D)
         Some of these girls don't even know what a Tampax is.

Maya stares at the two Thai girls on the bed. The Thai girl approaches Maya.

                         INDIAN GIRL (CONT'D)
          You have blue eyes. They are the eyes of an angel. My mother was
          raped by an Englishman. They are the eyes of a devil.

Another INDIAN GIRL lying on the bed sits up as if coming out of a stupor.

                         GIRL ON BED
          The girls they took away two nights ago, they said they were
          going to take care of rich peoples' children.

A number of the girls look around, waiting for someone to acknowledge their
hope. Maya turns toward the gated window.

Car headlights highlight Maya's face against the wall of the hotel room.

EXT. EXPRESSWAY - SAME

Tess makes a turn at a dilapidated hotel sign and parks the vehicle.

DRIVEWAY

A battered truck sits to the left of the parking lot.

A young INDIAN works under the open hood. Keith steps out from the shadows of a
doorway.

                              TESS
          Where are the girls?

                              KEITH
          Ah, yes, the girls. James called just a few minutes ago, said to
          give you the grand tour. Where is your cameraman?

                              TESS
          I'm going to make sure that the police ask you that question.

Keith walks ahead of Tess into the building, past the empty lobby and down a
narrow corridor.

                              TESS
          Were you working for Guardian when you kidnapped the girl and
          killed her father, or was that freelance?

                              KEITH
          He reneged on a deal. She was not his daughter. He bought her.
          When we came to pick her up, he tried to kill me.

Through open doors, a number of beds are in disarray, strewn with colorful
clothes and half-packed bags. Nine GIRLS, most of them seated on the floor.

Keith stands as a buffer between the girls and Tess.

                         KEITH (CONT'D)
          Girls, I'd like you to meet a friend of ours the Tiger lady.

The girls stare at Tess.

PARKING LOT

Bihari walks out toward the two men by the truck.

Keith says a few words, which are not heard and walks back into the hotel.

Maya, trancelike, takes a few steps toward Tess.

                              TESS
          Hello. How are you?

BATHROOM

A YOUNG MAN in black trousers, with a doctor's bag and a stethoscope dangling, comes out of the next room followed by a GIRL who is adjusting the waist string of her jalwari pants.

Tess leaves the cluster and walks across toward the doctor.

                              DOCTOR
          Mataji, I've got to rush. You can tell Mr. James that I will get
          the lab report to him first thing tomorrow morning.

The doctor heads toward Keith.

The doctor veers toward an old WOMAN cooking, grabs a fresh chapati, and offers one to Tess, who refuses.

The doctor walks quickly, exiting the room. Tess follows him as they exit the building.

                              TESS
          The girls?

                              DOCTOR
          All are HIV negative, and all but two are virgins. The only hands
          that have touched their delicate pink flowers are mine.

Abruptly he turns away, moving hastily towards his motorcycle.

ROW OF CARS

Tess opens the Mercedes door, hoping to find the key still in the ignition. It's not there.

A weathered pick-up truck sits in the foreground with the engine running erratically, creating a plume of thick, black smoke.

The doctor speeds away.

Tess removes her cell phone and dials a number. The phone RINGS and rings. Finally an answer.

                              TESS
          Yes, I'm at the Star Dust. I would like to speak with...

Gravel CRUNCHES behind her.

Tess cautiously moves her other hand to the back of her jacket, slowly removing
Dylan's revolver.

She quickly turns with the gun pointed at Keith's midsection.

PORCH OF MOTEL

The girls behind become unsettled.

Keith turns in an attempt to calm them, while at the same time assuages Tess.

                              KEITH
          Nothing to worry about (motioning to his accomplices). You're not
          going to shoot anyone.

Two other MEN approach on her left side.

                              KEITH (CONT'D)
          But you are scaring the hell out of these poor girls.

                              TESS
          You are buying and selling human beings?

                              KEITH
          Give me the gun before someone gets hurt.

Tess positions herself so that she can see all three men.

                              TESS
          It's over!

Keith continues toward her, his hand stretched out to her in a comical begging
gesture.

Another HOOD moves quietly behind Tess.

Tess turns and with one shot drops the other hood.

                              KEITH
          Son of a bitch!

                              TESS
          One down, three to go.

Bihari grabs her arm and shoulder from behind and tries to pull the gun from her
grasp.

Tess and Bihari struggle, a SHOT goes off.

Tess turns quickly, pointing the gun at Keith and Bihari; they turn with hands
held in the air.

                         TESS (CONT'D)
     The keys to the fucking truck!

Tess points the gun at Keith's head.

                         KEITH
     Give her the fucking keys!

Bihari tosses her the keys.

                         TESS
     Maya, tell the girls to get into the truck.

The girls stand looking at her as if she is an apparition. Maya steps forward.

                         TESS (CONT'D)
     Tell them to get in the back of the truck!

Maya turns slowly and repeats in Indian what Tess has just said. A few of the
girls head for the truck.

One of the girls suddenly deviates from the group and approaches Keith.

                         INDIAN GIRL
                        (Hindi dialect)
     I can't go home. They will kill me!

Bihari looks at her then back at Keith.

                         KEITH
     Did you hear what she said?

MOMENTS LATER

Maya walks toward the passenger door.

                         KEITH (CONT'D)
     You're risking your life and theirs. Girls that nobody cares are
     missing. You don't get it. They care more about their fucking
     cattle.

Tess fires a number of SHOTS. Keith and Bihari drop to the ground.

PARKING LOT - MOMENTS LATER

Keith gets to his feet.

Tess opens the driver door and gets in. She turns to fire. CLICK, CLICK, the gun
is empty.

TRUCK

Tess shifts into reverse, into drive and speeds away.

Keith FIRES a number of rounds at her vehicle as it speeds onto the rural highway.

Bihari comes back out of the building carrying a rifle. MERCEDES

Keith and Bihari get into the Mercedes.

EXT. RURAL ROAD - MOMENTS LATER

The truck has stalled. Maya sits in the front and plays with the choke. Finally, the truck starts again.

Bihari is at the wheel of the Mercedes as it pulls out onto the roadway to give chase. Keith sits in the passenger seat, gun drawn, another vehicle pulls up behind them.

EXT. TRUCK - CONTINUOUS

The truck bounces hard against the uneven roadway. Some of the girls in the back tumble over. Some are CRYING.

REAR VIEW MIRROR

Tess sees Keith's vehicle. Maya slides down into the seat as bullets shatter the windshield.

MERCEDES

Keith leans out of the window and empties a clip at the fleeing truck.

TRUCK

The girls take cover.

MERCEDES

Keith tries to pass them, but Tess cuts him off.

TRUCK

More shots are FIRED. Tess hits a large pothole in the road. The truck veers to the right and Keith SLAMS his vehicle alongside.

MERCEDES

A MAN in the rear of the Mercedes tries to climb onto the side of the truck.

TRUCK

The man stands on the rear bumper as two of the girls beat at him.

Bihari puts another clip in his pistol and begins FIRING.

The truck lunges to the left, SLAMMING into the side of the Mercedes. Keith fights to maintain control.

A decrepit stone bridge comes into view.

OTHER SIDE OF BRIDGE

Seconds later, the truck flies over the bridge. Keith's vehicle bounces off the stone walls of the bridge, hitting an open ditch and CRASHING into a construction vehicle, it bursts into flames.

Keith frees himself from the burning vehicle.

ROADWAY

Some hundred yards away, Tess descends from the cab of the truck as the Mercedes EXPLODES into flames.

TRUCK

Maya watches Tess climb out of the truck, gun in hand.

Maya walks slowly around the front of the burning vehicle stepping backwards toward the roadside foliage.

Girls climb out of the rear of the truck, a few stand trance-like on the roadway.

Bihari stands at the open door of the truck with gun in hand, bleeding profusely from a glass shard that is sticking out from his shirt.

Tess points the gun at Keith and fires. CLICK, the gun is empty.

                              KIT
          Do you know what that vehicle cost?

Bihari falls to the ground, the shard of glass poking out of his back.

Tess stands frozen as Keith walks toward her, gun in hand.

INT. MOUNTAIN HOTEL - TWO DAYS LATER

Tess lies in the corner of the room, her hands and feet tied. The room is cluttered with props from old Thai movie sets.

Several young MEN build what looks like a temple structure, part of a stage set.

One CARPENTER works on the interior frame of the set piece, reinforcing one of the corners with what looks like a wooden drawer.

                              TESS
          I need something to drink.

Keith violently goes through the room KICKING over cans and bottles. He picks up
a used water bottle.

She opens her mouth. He pours the water out onto the floor. Then HITS her.

DOORWAY

                              TESS (CONT'D)
          You son of a bitch.

James comes up from behind and pulls Keith away. James RIPS a piece of duct tape
from a roll.

                         JAMES
          Your story was over. You saw the girl you were looking for. She
          is alive. You know what they were doing and where they are going.
          You and your camera man shot the interview and get your ten
          minutes on the internet and MSNBC.

                         TESS
          My camera man is dead! You had him killed!

James looks at Keith, who is obviously coked up, pacing around behind him and
wanting to get his hands on her.

Tess struggles as he covers her mouth.

James pulls her up by to a standing position.

                    JAMES (SOFTLY) (CONT'D)
          This is much more than a bus load of girls in traffic and your
          ten minute spot on CNN.

                         KEITH
          Look at the rage in her eyes.

James looks at Keith, surmising that things may soon get out of control.

                      KEITH (CONT'D)
          She knows who you are, what we do.

She may even know about... I should have handed her over to some of the boys. It
gives me goose bumps to think what they would have done to you.

                         JAMES
          Shut the fuck up and get the truck!

EXT. REAR OF BUILDING - PARKING AREA- MOMENTS LATER

James walks Tess to the rear of a truck. Keith follows.

                         JAMES (softly)
          There are times in our lives when the magnitude of a situation
          makes one expendable.

Tess looks at James curiously.

                              TESS
          Fuck you!

James reaches into her pant's pockets and finds nothing. Then reaches around
into her jacket pocket and pulls out a cell phone along with a memory stick. He
puts both devices in his pocket. He picks Tess up and puts her in the rear of
the truck.

REAR OF TRUCK

James reaches into the bed of the truck and picks up a tin of gasoline and
loosens the top.

Keith tosses in an old wooden chair and a roll of duct tape.

She struggles, kicking Keith hard in the chest. Keith SMACKS Tess and she falls
back, knocking the can over, spilling the gasoline on Tess.

Keith takes his finger and strokes the side of Tess's cheek. With his fingertip,
he places a red dot just above her eyes, centered on her forehead.

Keith quickly flashes his lighter and moves to ignite the trail of gasoline in
the bed of the truck. James grabs his hand.

                              JAMES
          We want no trace of her. Start the fucking truck.

Keith walks around to the driver's side and climbs in. Tess lies motionless in
the rear of the truck.

                         JAMES (CONT'D)
          I hope that you live long enough to understand why I've done this.

James quickly douses the rest of Tess's body in gasoline.

INT. TRUCK - MOMENTS LATER

With his arm hanging outside the truck window, James clicks Tess's cell phone
taking pictures as they drive.

James pulls the cell phone back in.

                              KEITH
          What the fuck are you doing?

James looks at Keith then clicks into her phone. He sees the photos she took of
him and Sam.

                              JAMES
          Her phone. Just checking to see who she may have contacted.

James finds a group of numbers and sends the photos he has taken. They pull off the road and the truck stops. James takes two more photos.

                              JAMES (CONT'D)
          Looks like nothing.

James tosses the phone into the foliage.

EXT. FOREST AREA - LATER THAT NIGHT

The thick jungle foliage blocks the pink stone that once was part of a Hindu temple.

Tess sits, duct-taped to a chair at the top of a short hill overlooking a marsh.

There is an uneasy silence to the night. Tess is suddenly WHACKED across the side of her body.

TIGER

The tiger turns and pushes Tess over, the chair falls down the slope about twenty feet onto the wet edge of the field.

Tess frantically tries to pull herself free as the tiger circles her again. The tiger approaches, growls, then sits down just a few feet away from her.

Tess wakes from a sleep as bats flutter through the jungle treetops. The tiger is gone.

EXT. JUNGLE ROAD - LATE NIGHT

A group of elephants are led across the roadway by a FATHER and his two SONS.

A police vehicle pulls to a stop.

EXT. POLICE VEHICLE - CONTINUOUS

Mila and Dylan exit the vehicle. Mila clicks through her cell phone. Showing images of the road and present location.

                              MILA
          This looks like the place.

Dylan has crossed the road and begins to climb through the path covered in vegetation.

                              MILA (CONT'D)
          Jennings, wait, you may need this.

Dylan turns around as Mila hands him a revolver.

Mila's car phone begins to ring. She turns and heads back toward the vehicle.

EXT. JUNGLE FOLIAGE

Dylan enters the jungle foliage with only the moonlight illuminating his way.

Tess lies motionless on the ground to the left of Dylan. The sound of feet on STONE.

Dylan finally sees her.

Dylan drops to the ground and removes the tape from her mouth. She gasps for air. He smells the gasoline on her clothes.

                    TESS
     I thought you were dead.

                    DYLAN
     They killed Remi. You don't smell so good.

                    TESS
     He wanted me to be found.

Dylan wipes the hair from her face. He pulls her into his arms and they kiss passionately.

A tiger emerges from the tall grass and saunters slowly in their direction.

Dylan and Tess turn and face the tiger. It pauses and GROWLS.

                    DYLAN
     Eye contact!

A tiger cub steps out of the grass and growls, turns and prances back to its mother.

Tess and Dylan back away, then turn and break into a run. TALL GRASS - MOMENTS LATER

Dylan and Tess stand frozen a few yards away from the tiger that is now majestically illuminated by the police vehicle's headlights.

VEHICLE

Mila steps from the vehicle, gun in hand, aimed at the tiger.

                    TESS
     Don't shoot!

The headlights turn the jungle into an iridescent green as the tiger returns to her lair.

INT. MILA'S VEHICLE - MOMENTS LATER

                    MILA
     Here put this on.

Tess removes her shirt and puts on Mila's jacket.

EXT. MILA'S VEHICLE - MOMENTS LATER

The police vehicle moves along the jungle highway.

                         MILA (CONT'D)
          Did Guardian ever talk to you about the Indonesians?

Tess shakes her head no.

MILA (CONT'D)

Did you see anything else going on?

Mila's vehicle pulls into the hotel with headlights off.

                         TESS
          They held me in a large room. Looked like a shop. They were
          building stuff.

Dylan stares at a silver bus, as two men with headgear and protective body armor
leave the vehicle.

                         DYLAN
          What do they have to do with finding the girls?

                         MILA
          Absolutely nothing.

EXT. MOUNTAIN HOTEL - MINUTES LATER

Mila, Tess and Dylan quietly exit the vehicle and head in the shadows toward the
hotel.

Headlights from another vehicle rake the treetops. Mila motions for a number of
other officers to move forward.

INT. HOTEL - DARKENED ROOMS

Juliet motions for a number of the girls to remain silent as Tess and Dylan pass
outside the hotel windows.

Tess steps around Dylan as two officers put handcuffs on two young Asian males,
their mouths already taped.

Tess walks slowly toward three young girls seated on the floor; one of them is
Maya.

Tess and Maya exchange a glance. Maya nods and smiles.

INT. HOTEL CORRIDOR - MOMENTS LATER

Mila and Tess burst through the door. One of the hoods goes for his gun and is
wasted by Mila.

Dylan exits down the hallway in the other direction.

EXT. REAR OF HOTEL - SAME

James works his way along the rear of the building, gun in hand.

INT. ADDITIONAL ROOMS - SAME

Tess and Mila search other rooms. A GUNMAN, pointing a rifle, blocks one of the doors. Mila drops him with a shot to the head.

Tess picks up the guy's gun from the floor and exits out the rear of the building. Mila enters a second room. Keith steps into the room and drops Mila with a shot to the chest

EXT. REAR OF YARD - SAME

James has made it to the edge of the yard.

Tess rounds the rear of the building. James and Tess face off, guns pointed at each other.

                    JAMES
          It looks like your dinner guest didn't show?

                    TESS
          My attire kind of left a bad taste in its mouth.

Keith comes up from behind and puts the gun to the side of Tess's head. Keith pulls the gun from her hand as Dylan approaches from the walkway.

                    DYLAN
          Let her go!

Dylan raises his revolver and fires but the gun is empty.

Keith turns and with the other pistol, FIRES hitting Dylan in the head.

                    TESS (SCREAMS)
          No, No! You son of a bitch!

                    KEITH
          Just like in the fucking movies.

Keith pushes the gun hard against Tess's head.

Police SIRENS can be heard as lights rake though the trees. Tess tries to pull away.

                    TESS
          Shoot him!

                              KEITH
          Pardon me, but I'm going to have to leave this lovely get
          together.

          The question is, do I take her along with me, or do you put your
          guns down so she--

                              TESS
          Shoot him!

                              JAMES
          Keith, it's over...let her go.

                              KEITH
          She is supposed to be dead!

Tess struggles as Keith pulls her tight against his body.

                              JAMES
          I said let her go.

                              KEITH
          Let's make a deal.

James lowers his pistol.

                              KEITH (CONT'D)
          You tell me who the fuck you really work for, and maybe I'll...

                              JAMES
          Only thing that matters is you have the merchandise and I have
          the money. Give her to me and...

                              KEITH
          But Jimmy, there's a slight hitch to our current scenario. I got
          a better offer!

Keith raises his other hand and hits James with two SHOTS. James fires as he
falls to the ground.

A number of police come out of the adjoining building. Tess breaks away from
Keith, bullets flying in both directions as Keith leaps off of the ravine into
the dense foliage below.

Tess slowly gets to her feet and walks toward Dylan who lies dead with a bullet
hole in his head.

Tess turns and heads toward James who looks as if death is but a breath away.

                              JAMES
          Are you okay?

Tess nods yes.

James's head rests in Tess's arms. He is now unconscious. Paramedics put Dylan's dead body onto a stretcher.

EXT. ROADWAY AND PARKING LOT - MINUTES LATER AMBULANCE

Two paramedics get out and head in their direction.

Tess picks up James's pistol and sticks it into the back of her pants as paramedics place James on the stretcher.

EXT. PARKING LOT - MOMENTS LATER

A full moon hangs over the distant Hotel.

Tess walks back toward the lot as additional POLICE and TV vehicles arrive, sirens BLARING.

A medium-sized bus with dark windows sits idling in the middle of the crowded parking lot.

BUS

Tess walks alongside the bus trying to see through the tinted windows.

Mookie exits the bus. He rolls down the hillside and slides under the open crawl space between one of the old buildings.

A CAMERA CREW climbs out of a news van.

Juliet exits the front of the hotel. A young female REPORTER approaches along with a cameraman and crew. Two COPS quickly approach.

> POLICE OFFICER
> Get your hands in the air. In the air! And don't make a move!

EXT. HOTEL ENTRANCE - SAME

A number of girls exit the hotel behind Juliet. One of them is Maya.

> REPORTER
> I'm not exactly sure what is going on here. Suspected terrorists, drug smugglers, there seem to be a number of young women on a bus, now leaving the bus. Some of them are crying. A man and two women. What? Tess who? I have just been told that the woman is ... yes, the woman has been identified as CNN correspondent, Tess Douglas.

The young female reporter approaches Juliet.

EXT. CNN HELICOPTER CIRCLES ABOVE

> JULIET
> You don't get it. You send these girls home. You might as well be signing their death certificates.

Tess reaches out and takes the microphone from the reporter's hand.

CENTER OF LOT

Tess points toward the young women and girls. The young reporter motions, the camera follows her direction.

                              TESS
          These are the real endangered species. The purchase and sale of
          human beings.

Tess walks along with the group of young girls assembled behind her, sweeping her arm inclusively as Maya separates from them and walks toward her.

Tess walks toward Maya, who has a warm appreciative look on her face. The chain medallion of the goddess and tiger that hangs around her neck now is clutched tightly in her hand. Tess removes the necklace and places it around Maya's neck.

Tess places the microphone in front of Maya.

                              MAYA
          We, the other girls and I, were being made into a dance troupe.
          They were making props for the performances, but we never learned
          to dance.

                              TESS
          Their names could be Kalpana, Tanya, Maria, U Ming or Maya. Just
          like your daughters full of life and eager to become young women.

EXT. CENTER OF LOT - SAME

Tess separates herself from Maya and from the continuing police activity. Her stance is strong and deliberate. Her voice gains in intensity as she holds Maya's hand and steps toward the camera.

The young female reporter approaches, she is not much older than some of the stolen girls.

                         TESS (CONT'D)
          Each of these young women represents a stolen life. A very small
          part of a worldwide network, a billion dollar industry that buys
          and sells human beings, the majority are female and under the age
          of 17. India, China, Cambodia, Romania, Mexico, Ethiopia, Brazil,
          India, Russia. The list goes on and on. Stolen, kidnapped, bought
          and sold like livestock.

Tess gives the microphone back to the reporter.

EXT. OVERVIEW PARKING LOT AND ROAD - SAME

An aerial view of the crash site from a circling helicopter.

Tess nods as Maya smiles and joins the other girls as they head toward one of the medical vehicles.

AMBULANCE

They are about to move Mila to an ambulance. Tess bends over and kisses Mila on the forehead.

                                        TESS
          Good cop.

Mila tries to smile.

                                        MILA
          Get out of here.

A second stretcher passes carrying Guardian's body. Juliet walks along side him.

A black limo pulls up behind Tess.

Inside the vehicle, SAM, an American early sixties, beard, 20 pounds overweight speaks to am ASIAN man, who steps out of the car along with Sam.

To their left, a number of men in protective uniforms, along with three dogs, leave their vehicles and walk toward the bus and hotel.

                                        SAM
          Fuck! Find out what happened to Guardian. I want Keith Dalton...
          alive.

James is loaded into an ambulance. Juliet climbs in after him.

Sam smiles as he walks toward Tess.

                                        SAM (CONT'D)
          Ms. Douglas, it's great to see you back on the air again. But this
          is not exactly the Discovery Channel.

                                        TESS
          And who the fuck are you?

Sam motions for her to follow him.

                                        SAM
          Let's just say a friend of the family... The guy who's supposed to
          get you safely out of here and back home. I'll take you to the
          airport.

Sam motions for her to get into the back of the vehicle.

OVERVIEW

A helicopter circles the hotel and arrest site.

INT. BLACK LIMO - MINUTES LATER

The black vehicle moves quickly along the rural highway.

                              SAM
          We got lucky here. Problem is what do we do with the girls now?
          Kind of the difference between wholesale and retail. It's a bitch,
          but these things happen. We did get your cameraman's tip about the
          auction. By the time the police got there, nothing left but a bunch
          of rich businessmen bonding over cricket, champagne, good cigars,
          and under-age pussy.

                              TESS
          Who ever the hell you work for... All this attention, the SWAT
          team response, the men wearing bomb protection outfits...

Tess looks out the car window, wishing she had not gotten in the vehicle.

                              TESS (CONT'D)
          What went down back there has very little to do with the sale of
          a bus load of females.

Sam stiffens slightly in the front seat and talks looking straight out the
windshield.

                              TESS (CONT'D)
          I know our government has been involved in the heroin and cocaine
          trade, but human trafficking...

                              SAM
          The black market is a multi-layered expressway. A labyrinth
          of multifaceted businesses -- drugs, consumer goods, women and
          weapons -- all interconnected through various trade routes and
          players.

                              TESS
          Was Guardian a spook?

                              SAM
          We were looking for Keith Dalton, a point-man, a connecting link
          with terrorist cells in both the Middle East and the Pacific Rim.
          As a side bar he was also one of the major traffickers in the
          flesh trade.

Sam lights a cigarette.

                              SAM (CONT'D)
          Do you mind?

Tess shakes her head no and then raises her hand asking for one.

                              TESS
          So the skin trade was Guardian's cover?

                              SAM
          Six months ago Guardian thought he had located a DB carrier. A
          dinner meeting with two men who claimed they had just purchased
          a small device, one that could fit in a suitcase, smuggled out of
          Indonesia. We were about to wire five million to an account in
          Jakarta.

                              TESS
          So the plan was to have it smuggled into the U.S. via a bogus dance
          troupe?

                              SAM
          Cultural, artistic-sponsored visas are very easy to get.

                              TESS
          Was it going to be used as ransom or--

                              SAM
          No. The plan was to take out a good portion of Manhattan.

Sam removes the BEEPING cell phone from his pocket.

                              SAM (CONT'D)
          And that is still the... Hello? Did they find it? Son of a bitch...
          They searched the fucking bus?

Sam's tone has suddenly changed as he turns and looks out at the oncoming
highway.

                              SAM (CONT'D)
          Your boyfriend, Guardian, is in serious but stable condition.

Sam rolls down the window tossing the cigarette.

                              SAM (CONT'D)
          No bomb and that English motherfucker seems to have vanished.

The DRIVER, a young Asian, pulls down the front sun visor, to look at himself in
the mirror.

Tess looks at the visor, a photo I.D. Card in an Asian font and a nation's flag.

The vehicle makes a turn onto another highway.

                              TESS (in Indonesian)
          The license plate on this vehicle is the Indonesian Embassy

The driver, seeming to be surprised, looks at Tess then at Sam. Sam turns
slightly and smiles.

Sam turns around as he puts on sun glasses and stares out the window.

Tess leans forward, exposing the small of her back and the gun stuck in the back
of her pants.

                              TESS (CONT'D)
          My only concern was trying to do something about the sale of
          human beings as if they are cattle.

Sam reaches forward and opens the glove compartment as the car, and removes a
revolver. The car slows down and pulls off to the side of the road.

                              TESS (CONT'D)
          So, is Guardian also working for the Indonesians?

EXT. RICE FIELDS - LATER THAT DAY

Mookie moves hurriedly through the rice field.

Twenty yards behind, the female tiger quietly follows him.

TIGER

Silently the tiger approaches, leaps and takes him down.

EXT. FIELD - MOMENTS LATER

The tiger drags Mookie through the rice field, followed by her two cubs.

EXT. ROADWAY - SAME

The black limo pulled off to the side of the road.

On the other side of the vehicle, Sam lies halfway out of the front door with a
bullet hole in his head. The driver lies dead against the steering wheel.

Tess removes Sam's cell and puts it in her pocket.

EXT. TWO LANE BLACKTOP - LATER THAT DAY.

A battered pick-up truck. The bed of the truck filled with birds in wood and
metal cages.

At the rear of the truck sits Tess, with Sam's cell phone gripped tightly in
her hand.

The truck continues down a two-lane highway toward the ominous metropolis of
Mumbai.

EXT. HARBOR LOADING DOCK - FIVE DAYS LATER - SUNSET.

A fancy school bus pulls into a loading dock. Keith gets out of this vehicle.

EXT. OTHER END OF LOT

Tess and Juliet climb out of a black Hummer.

Keith walks toward them, his left arm hangs in a blood-stained shoulder sling.

LOADING DOCK

Nothing is said as they walk along the dock area toward an open container.

                              KEITH
          Too bad about Guardian.

The container is empty. A porta-san rests at the far end. Rows of plywood sleeping bunks fill the rest of the space.

                         KEITH (CONT'D)
          Where are they?

Juliet smiles. Keith gives her a cold stare.

                              JULIET
          No birds today. We had a problem.

Suddenly a heavy downpour begins. They all climb into the container.

                              KEITH
          What the fuck do I tell our client? How long have you known this?
          Thefucking container...it's... Wait until Sam hears about this...He
          will have you two cunts...

Keith walks further inside the container and makes a phone call on his cell phone.

                         KEITH (CONT'D)
          It's me. There is no… Sam? What?.. He is fucking dead?

Keith looks at Tess and Juliet. Tess smiles and motions with her finger like a gun to her head, and silently mouths "bang, bang." She now points her hand as gun toward Keith.

                              KEITH
          Okay, Okay… Shut the fuck up and listen. I need twenty-five girls,
          ASAP. Are you listening?… I need cherries, nothing older than 17.
          I need them in three fucking days. I don't care how you get them!
          Fuck, I have to take a piss. Fuck! Fuck!

Keith, screaming obscenities, heads toward the porta-san at the rear of the container.

As he opens the stall door, there is an impact at the top of the container, and it shifts slightly.

Keith looks up and back out toward the front of the container. Tess and Juliet are now standing outside the still open container.

                              KEITH
          No, no… You stupid cunts!

Juliet and Tess close the door of the container. Juliet and Tess walk back toward the Hummer. Juliet tosses Keith's cell phone into the water. Pounding and screaming can be heard as the container is lifted into the air.

EXT. HUMMER

The driver's side tinted window slowly goes down. James, now with a short beard and darker hair, sits looking as the container rises over the deck of a freighter. He has a cellphone to his ear as Juliet and Mia approach. The car window goes up as he begins talking on the cell phone.

INT. CAR

                              JAMES
          This is Sam Ford... No, Mr. Dalton, has had to take a sudden trip
          to Australia, needed some R&R... . Guardian canceled the meeting.

The passenger side door of the car opens.

                       JAMES (CALM VOICE)
          We know longer have to worry about Guardian. He is dead... Yes, I
          am the other interested buyer...Stop... Listen and please listen
          very carefully. I do not like to repeat myself. We will meet in
          Delhi in three days. I will contact you concerning the time and
          location tomorrow. The money will be wired when I have been given
          the merchandise.

James looks at Tess who is now seated next to him.

                        JAMES (CONT'D)
          And please no more middlemen.

James clicks off the cell phone and turns toward Tess, Juliet is now in the back seat.

                              TESS
          So, James Guardian is now history.

                             JULIET
          The storyline is he died four days ago during a raid on a sex
          trafficking ring.

                      TESS (LOOKING AT JULIET)
          What side of the tracks was he on?

James stares out the car window and says nothing.

                             JULIET
          It was a fatwah. Guardian was shot by one of the traffickers who
          suspected he was working with the police.

James turns and nods towards Juliet. James turns toward Tess and places his hand on her thigh as Juliet gets out the rear door. There is an airplane ticket in his hand.

                              JAMES
This time, you will be taken to the airport and flown back to the States.

          She reluctantly takes the ticket.

                              TESS
          How do I get a hold of you?

Tess is startled as her door is opened from the outside by Juliet. James shakes
his head no.

                              JAMES
          You don't! If needed, it will be much easier for me to find you.

                              TESS
          Where is this meeting taking place?

                              JAMES
          What meeting?

                              TESS
          You do remember what I do for a living?

James leans over and kisses her as Juliet grabs Tess's arm and firmly removes her
from the car. Tess pulls away from her but follows. James leans toward the window.

                              JAMES
          Not to steal your punch line but...the most important thing for
          you to do right now is to remember what I do and the monsters
          that I do business with…what I do for a living.

James puts on his shades. They smile at each other. The window goes up as James's
vehicle slowly pulls away.

INT. HUMMER- MOMENTS LATER

Juliet in the driver's seat, Tess now in the back seat. They exchange a glance.
Tess nods "yes," as she closes the glass window dividing the front seat from the
back. The vehicle pulls away as Tess takes out her cell phone and dials.

                              TESS
          Hello? it's Tess Douglas... Yes, I'm fine, thank you. Can I speak
          with Alex Anderson?

As she is waiting for a response Tess notices a folded map of Jakarta stuffed in
the back seat.

                              TESS
          Okay, can you tell her to please call me...I have a story.

Moments later Tess looks out the window as the vehicle approaches the airport

Close up of the resolve on Tess's face.

MOMENTS LATER

The sliding between the front and back seat jerks open. Juliet and Tess exchange a look in the rearview mirror.

                              JULIET
          I'm sure you're going to put everything, heart and soul, into this
          shocking story. It may even get you a seat on late-night talk
          or morning news shows. (CLOSE UP REFLECTION IN MIRROR) Just the
          tip of the iceberg. Do not forget where many of these girls came
          from, that many are sold by their families. My father sold me for
          a TV and a cable feed. He wanted to watch fucking *Baywatch* had a
          thing for big tits and string bikinis.

Their vehicle jerks to a stop.

Juliet turns from the mirror and looks at Tess face-to-face.

                              JULIET
          Many of these girls actually choose this as a means to support
          their families or get a sweatshop factory job.

Tess looks again at the Jakarta map. Juliet adjusts herself to see what Tess is looking at.

                         JULIET (CONT'D)
          Sam used this vehicle. We just started to do some new business in
          Jakarta. I doubt that contact is on your list.

                              TESS
          I realize that many of these girls actually choose this as a
          means to support their families, or get a sweatshop factory job.

Juliet smiles and licks her lips.

                              JULIET
          He is aware of the information that you have. If and when you do your
          story...(SHE PUCKERS HER DEEP RED LIPS) Mr. Guardian remains a deadman.

They stare at each other as Tess goes to open the car door.

                         JULIET (CONT'D)
          My dear Tiger lady...Isn't that what she called you? Whatever it
          is you think you know about James' other business, it would be a
          very good idea for you to have amnesia. It is way above both of
          our pay scales. And again, if you mention either James or my name
          in any of your news stories to any novel storylines, the Tiger
          Lady's life expectancy will be...Extinct.

Tess closes the car door. Juliet does not look back as the Hummer speeds away. Tess pauses as she takes out her ticket, then begins to walk toward the terminal. She stops and looks at the list of airlines posted on a monitor and then back at her ticket.

                              TESS
          FUCK!

EXT. THREE DAYS LATER:

Overview of an extremely crowded urban area. Many people on bicycles, scooters.
Street shops line the side streets. Close-up of women wearing headscarves. Large
luxury hotel in foreground.

A woman wearing shimmering blue slacks, a black silk blazer, and a floral head
scarf walks toward the hotel entrance.

Walkway with stone-carved sign, same name as the hotel on the business card in
the car.

INT. HOTEL ENTRANCE

Businessmen, tourists, and young hotel staff fill the lobby. Fancy coffee shop.
This same woman is now seated and talking with a very young female waitress.

OVERVEIW OF BUSY LOBBY.

CLOSE UP.

The same woman's hands are fluttering like wings as she is typing on a laptop,
pulling up numerous files and folders, faster than they can be read, and attaching
them to an email address. Done, she sends the email and closes the laptop.

The waitress carefully places the cappuccino on the table.

CLOSE UP of the ASIAN TEENAGE WAITRESS'S beautiful smiling face.

From the back of the table, the woman nods and removes her scarf. She shakes
her blonde hair and concentrates on the lobby and front reception desk in front
of her. The woman looks at the foam that rests on the surface of the drink. The
waitress had drawn in foam the head of a tiger.

With her face in full view, Tess takes a sip, turns her head and gives a confident
smile.

FADE OUT

Garey Riester is an American contemporary Post-War artist based
in both Easton, Pennsylvania and New York City. Known for his var-
ied style and prolific photorealist exploration of the mediums of
painting and drawing, he combines aesthetics of immediacy, the
essence of nature and personal narrative to study and affect the
world around him. Throughout his career, Riester has exhibited in
various galleries and museums and his work is represented in a number of public and private collections. He has been making art for
more than 65 years and writing for the past 30 years. His screenplays have won numerous awards at film and screenplay festivals.
He now lives with his dog Walter in Easton, Pa.